*Introduction*

Thank you for your interest in my illustrated novella. Before you get into it, there are just two things I would like to point out. Firstly, this is a standalone novella, but it is also a part of a trilogy of novellas, which together tell an overarching story. And secondly, this novella has no chapters; the story is instead divided into two-page sections, of which there are a total of twenty-six. Some other information, such as how this novella came into being, can be found in the *Author's Note*, at the very end of this book.

Tristaria Volume 1: Of Palantaros

1st Standard Edition

© Maruse Rino 2021

ISBN: 978-0-6450787-0-1

# TRISTARIA

## VOLUME 1: OF PALANTAROS

An Illustrated Novella by Maruse Rino

# TRISTARIA

*In* the great southern region, known as Lianthia to its inhabitants, autumn had arrived. However, on the subtropical islands of the Kien Archipelago, which lay off the northern shores of Lianthia, it never really grew cold, not even in the middle of winter. And so it was here, on a tiny sun-blessed island known as Kien Taril, that the temple dedicated to Altaris, the Sun Goddess, was located. This ancient but resplendent temple was home to the Priestesses of Altaris, whose renown as healers was second to none in all of Lianthia.

It was now late afternoon and the sun hung low in the sky, casting a soft yellow glow on the land below, but it was still quite warm. Tristaria was alone, busily sweeping a narrow stone path in a secluded corner of the temple. The path, flanked by a large building on one side and the outer wall of the temple on the other, was quite long, but Tristaria had nearly finished clearing it of dust and debris. Around her, all was quiet. Apart from the soft sound of her broom brushing against the flagstones at her bare feet, and the occasional cry of distant sea birds, there were no sounds.

Although Tristaria lived in the Temple of Altaris, she was not a priestess. The priestesses had no time for menial tasks such as sweeping. That work was done by the novices; hopeful young girls who were studying at the temple in order to one day possibly become priestesses themselves. And that is what Tristaria was: a novice. She wore a plain, white cotton outfit consisting of a bralette and loincloth, as all novices did. The purpose of this outfit was to keep the wearer as cool as possible in the hot climate of Kien Taril, but even so, Tristaria's clothing was damp with perspiration, and it clung to her slender frame so that her dark brown skin was partially visible through it.

Apart from these cotton garments, the only other things Tristaria wore were a thin leather headband, which kept her long golden hair from falling over her bright violet eyes, and a choker necklace, from which hung a bright, tear-shaped jewel. Generally, jewellery and other such adornments were not permitted in the Temple of Altaris, but there were some exemptions. In Tristaria's case, she was allowed to wear her necklace because it was a memento of her mother.

Soon, a woman came around the far corner of the building. She was taller than Tristaria, and much older, with slightly tanned skin and long straight hair that was greying. Unlike Tristaria, she was dressed in a long tunic and had sandals on her feet. She also wore a golden medallion around her neck. This medallion identified her as none other than the high priestess of the Temple. Her name was Lusianis.

Upon catching sight of Tristaria, Lusianis called out to her. "Tristaria!" she said.

Tristaria looked at the older woman. "Yes, mistress?" she answered.

"May I have a quick word with you?"

"Yes of course, mistress."

Lusianis approached the spot where Tristaria was standing. "Thank you, my child. I know it's been a long hard day for you, so I will make this brief."

Tristaria frowned slightly. "Is there something amiss, mistress?"

The high priestess gave a slight chuckle and then shook her head. "No, there's nothing amiss. I just wanted to let you know that your chanting today was splendid. You have well and truly attuned yourself to the power of Lady Altaris!"

A bashful smile appeared on Tristaria's lips. "Thank you, mistress. It pleases me to hear you say so."

Lusianis went on. "You almost certainly have the potential to be a great asset to the temple one day, Tristaria."

"But... But nothing is certain yet, is it mistress? I mean, I still have to pass my final trial this winter, don't I?"

"Of course! I just wanted to remind you to keep up the good work. Don't think that just because the end is in sight that you can relax. On the contrary, now is the time for you to put in as much effort as you can. Do that, and you will have an excellent chance of fulfilling your dream of becoming a healer here."

Tristaria found it hard to suppress her glee, but she somehow managed to do so. "Thank you for your words of advice, high priestess. I will not forget them."

"I know you won't, my child. Now, I think I have taken up enough of your time. Good evening."

"Good evening, mistress."

As Lusianis departed and Tristaria was left alone once more, the young girl could no longer contain herself. A broad smile appeared on her face and her eyes sparkled with joy. Even though Tristaria had aspired to join the Priestesses of Altaris for most of her life, not until now had she felt that this dream was within reach.

# TRISTARIA

*O*nce Tristaria had put away the broom in the storeroom, where it belonged, she headed to the Novice's Quarters, which was a long low building near the western wall of the temple.

By this time, dusk had set in and the sky was growing dark. Several other novices were also headed to the Novice's Quarters; these girls were all dressed like Tristaria, but unlike her, most of them had fair skin and dark hair. Tristaria exchanged brief but pleasant words with a few of them on the way to her private room.

The rooms occupied by the novices of the temple, who were officially only in the temple temporarily, were very small. They did not even have doors, just a curtained doorway, and they were sparsely furnished: the only furniture they had was a bunk, a table, a stool and a set of shelves, all of which were made of wood. The bunk did have a mattress, but it was only stuffed with straw. In fact, the only thing about the novice's rooms that could be considered at all luxurious was that they each had their own small stone baths. As for personal belongings, the only items novices were allowed to keep in their rooms were generally related to the study of magic, and in particular, healing magic. Chief among these, of course, were their magic staffs, but also included such things as books and medicinal herbs. Any superfluous belongings novices might have brought with them to the temple, such as valuables, were kept in the storeroom.

When Tristaria stepped into her room, it was quite dark. There were a number of small windows just under the ceiling on the rear wall, but they primarily served to allow fresh air inside, and were not really for providing light. So the first thing Tristaria did was light the candle that sat on her little wooden table. It was not a very big candle, but it gave off a surprisingly bright glow. This was because it had been manufactured in the temple, and it had been infused with magical properties.

Her room now well-illuminated, Tristaria set about her usual evening routine, which consisted almost entirely of studying. She did, however, have to take a break from studying to eat dinner. But since the food was brought to her doorway by the novices whose chore it was to cook for that day, she did not need to leave her room for this.

After she was finished studying, the last thing that Tristaria would do everyday was take a bath. She enjoyed this time of day, especially in summer. It felt wonderful to wash away the perspiration and dust that somehow managed to cake itself onto her skin every single day. Also, the herbs that she had been given to use in the bath were incredibly fragrant and soothed her tired body, as well as her tired mind. Thanks to the bath, she was always able to sleep well.

Night had well and truly fallen when Tristaria carefully stood up and stepped out from her bath. Water streamed down her naked body as she reached for her towel, which she had left on her stool, and with it she proceeded to gently dab her skin dry. It was at that moment when she heard a loud fluttering, like that of a bird, although it was most likely not a bird, because it was nighttime.

Feeling a little unnerved, Tristaria clutched the towel close to the front of her body and looked towards the little windows below the ceiling, as this was the direction the sound had come from. There, obscured in shadow, a small creature sat. It looked very much like a cat, but one with wings. The creature squawked and Tristaria's eyes opened wide in surprise, for it was a squawk she recognized.

"Eramaklis!" she cried out.

The creature stood up on four legs and walked along the window sill, towards Tristaria and closer to the candlelight, becoming more visible. It was a faerie-gryphon. Its head and upper body were that of a crested hawk, whilst its lower body, including its tail, was that of a cat. Its plumage and fur were both entirely reddish brown in colour, apart from the dark stripes on its back and tail.

"Greetings, Tristaria," Eramaklis said, in a deep, mellow voice. "It has been quite a long time since we last met, has it not?"

"It certainly has," Tristaria agreed. Eramaklis had been the constant companion of her former teacher, the great wizard Aldoranis, who had passed away over two years ago.

"Have you been well, Tristaria?"

"Yes, very well. I trust you have been well also?"

"Yes. For the most part."

"And Palantaros? Do you know how he is? Not in trouble, I hope." Tristaria said this in jest, which was evident by the grin on her face, but Eramaklis said nothing in response. After a few moments, Tristaria let out a deep sigh. "Of course he's in trouble," she said, answering her own question. "That's the reason you're here, isn't it?"

Eramaklis nodded. "I promised Aldoranis that I would look after Palantaros in his place, but Palantaros certainly has a knack for getting himself into all sorts of difficult situations."

Tristaria groaned and her head dropped. "That sounds just like the Palantaros I know," she said, but her voice was now very quiet, as if she was talking to herself, rather than the small creature near her.

Tristaria's thoughts drifted back several years earlier, when she and Palantaros had both been apprentices to Aldonaris. Palantaros was quite talented in the use of magic, as in fact all of Aldonaris' pupils were, but he was hopeless when it came to studying. He much preferred to go out and cause mischief. And since Tristaria was younger than he was, she would often foolishly go along with his silly games and pranks, but the two of them would invariably end up in trouble. Afterwards, Tristaria would be so angry at Palantaros because of this. However, they were both merely children at the time. What more could you expect? She had hoped, of course, that Palantaros had matured somewhat during the time that they had been apart. But it now looked like that hope had been in vain.

Tristaria looked back up at Eramaklis. "So, what's happened to Palantaros this time?" she asked. And Eramaklis told her.

# TRISTARIA

*Tristaria* moved hurriedly through the moonlit central courtyard of the temple. She had put on a short cotton nightdress, but she was barefoot and her hair was still fairly damp from her recent bath. She did not bother following any of the gravel paths; she headed straight across the grass towards the arched entrance to the Priestesses' Quarters.

The Priestesses' Quarters was a huge building. It was three levels high and divided into two wings, with a staircase in the middle. It completely dwarfed the Novice's Quarters and, aside from the Grand Hall and the Main Library, it was probably the largest building on the temple grounds.

As Tristaria bounded up the staircase, she overtook a pair of priestesses who were also on their way up. One of them gave a stifled gasp, which did not surprise Tristaria. Novices were not usually allowed to enter the Priestesses' Quarters, even during the day; during the night, it was practically forbidden.

Upon reaching the third floor, Tristaria turned into the east hallway. Although the hallway had no windows, just a number of doors, it was well-lit by several oil lamps that hung from the ceiling. The high priestesses' room, Tristaria's destination, was at the far end of the hallway. When Tristaria reached it, she wasted no time in knocking on the door, softly but firmly. There was a response almost immediately. "Please come in," the voice of the high priestess said.

Tristaria entered the room, which was rather dimly lit, and quickly closed the door behind her. It had been a while since she had last been here, but it was just as she remembered it: large, but cluttered. There were numerous cabinets and shelves, all of them completely filled with either jars and bottles, or books and scrolls.

Lusianis was sitting at her table, a quill in her hand. Although she was facing the door, her attention was firmly fixed on a rolled-out scroll in front of her. Several other scrolls lay scattered about on the table, some also rolled-out, some not, suggesting that she was in the middle of some important research. A lamp hanging from the wall near her was the only source of light in the room. Tristaria hovered nervously by the door for a few moments, unsure if she should announce herself or not, but before she could say anything, Lusianis glanced up at her.

"Tristaria!" she exclaimed, her face filled with shock.

"I'm sorry to disturb you, mistress, but you see—" Tristaria began to say, but the high priestess was still not over her shock.

"What are you doing here? And why are you not presentable?"

Tristaria took a moment to collect her thoughts. She knew this was not going to be easy, so she decided the best thing to do was to get straight to the point. Tristaria's face turned deathly serious. "Mistress, I need your permission to leave the temple," she said. "Tonight."

For a moment, the high priestess stared agape at the young girl, but she soon regained her composure. "What is this all about, Tristaria?"

"I just received a message, via a faerie-gryphon, about a dear friend of mine. A boy named Palantaros. He's in trouble and he needs my help."

Lusianis appeared slightly perplexed. "Please elaborate."

Tristaria took a deep breath and began to relate the story that Eramaklis had told her, moments earlier.

"Well, mistress, Palantaros has been imprisoned by King Galasius of Taraminas, on Kien Sifel. It seems that while he was performing a magical show in the main square, he accidentally set fire to an orchard. The king's orchard. Quite a number of trees were damaged and many apples lost. The king fined him one hundred gold coins for this, but unfortunately, Palantaros cannot pay the fine. So he was imprisoned. And unless he can find a way to pay the fine within three days, he will receive a public beating."

Lusianis looked at Tristaria silently for a few moments. "That is indeed unfortunate news," she said, at length.

"Then I have your permission?" Tristaria said, a faint smile of hope appearing on her lips.

"No," the high priestess responded.

"But—"

"Listen to me, Tristaria. Whatever happened on Taraminas has nothing to do with you. That boy Palantaros got himself into a mess and now he must get himself out of it. It's as simple as that."

"But he doesn't have the money to pay the fine!" Tristaria protested.

"Do you?"

"No, but if I talk to the king, maybe…" Tristaria trailed off.

"Oh, I know King Galasius, and he's a good man, but very hard-headed. I doubt you will be able to convince him to let your friend go just like that."

"But—"

"And do I have to remind you of what I told you earlier today? This is when you need to concentrate on what you are doing here the most! Don't jeopardize your future by allowing yourself to be distracted by things that are beyond your control."

Tristaria lowered her gaze, defeated.

Lusianis' expression softened slightly. "Tristaria, you are a very compassionate girl," she said soothingly. "You have a strong desire to help all those who need it. That is one of the reasons you have been able to attune yourself so well to Lady Altaris. However, it is a sad fact of life that you will never be able to help everybody. There are times when you will be unable to do anything. This is one of them. Do you understand what I'm saying, Tristaria?"

After a long pause, Tristaria nodded slowly, keeping her eyes on the floor before her. "Yes," she replied. "I understand, mistress."

The high priestess smiled. "Good."

# TRISTARIA

*W*hen Tristaria returned to her room, Eramaklis was sitting on her table, patiently waiting for her. "So how did it go?" he asked.

Tristaria said nothing, but her dejected expression told the faerie-gryphon all he needed to know.

"Not well, it would appear," Eramaklis concluded.

"Not well at all," Tristaria said sadly, and she went over to her bunk and sat down on it, heavily.

"Do not feel too bad, Tristaria. Palantaros will understand. Before I left him, I warned him it was highly unlikely that you would be allowed to leave the temple."

Tristaria slowly drew one of her knees up towards her chin, then rested both of her arms on it. "Maybe... Maybe I can sneak out," Tristaria suggested, but there was little conviction in her words.

"No, Tristaria. That won't be necessary. I have another option."

"And what is that?"

"I will go to Port Kerastes. I know that Miralena is working there, at a potion shop," Eramaklis said. He was referring to another of Aldoranis' former pupils, who Tristaria knew quite well. "I will go to talk to her and see if she can help."

"Port Kerastes?" Tristaria repeated slowly. "How long will it take you to get there?"

"No more than two days."

"Two days? That means you won't be back in Taraminas until four days from now. That's after the beating is scheduled to take place!"

"The trip back from Kerastes will be shorter. Remember, Taraminas lies south of Kien Taril. There's a good chance that I'll make it back in time."

"But that's assuming Miralena is where you think she is. And even then won't she need time to get to Taraminas herself?"

"It certainly won't be straightforward, I know. But I believe things will work out in the end, somehow."

"I hope you're right..."

"Only time will tell. But I'm afraid I must now bid you farewell, Tristaria, as I must hurry. It was a pleasure to speak to you again. Good luck with your studies." With that, Eramaklis beat his wings furiously and quickly flew out of Tristaria's room.

No sooner had the faerie-gryphon left, that Tristaria jumped on top of her bunk and stood on the tips of her toes, so that she could look out through the little windows in her room. "Give my greetings to Palantaros!" she yelled out, towards the small shadow in the night sky that was gracefully arcing towards the south.

"I shall!" came the reply. Then Eramaklis vanished.

Tristaria sullenly stepped down from her bunk and went over to the candle. With a quick puff of air from her lips, the candle went out and the room was filled with eerie, moon-cast shadows. She returned to her bunk, lay down on it and pulled a thin blanket over her body. Then she tried to get to sleep.

But she could not sleep. She had trouble even keeping her eyes shut. Naturally, her thoughts centred on Palantaros. At first, she recalled the many times that he had gotten her into trouble by convincing her to join him in his crazy escapades. She made an effort to use the anger that those memories resurrected to ease the guilt she now felt at abandoning Palantaros at his time of need. But then she remembered something else. A memory from when she had first arrived at Aldoranis' tower, the place where both she and Palantaros had started studying magic.

Tristaria had always been a very curious child, and the great old wizard Aldoranis had many a thing stored in his tower that captivated her. This included those that were forbidden to her and the other apprentices, such as the All-seeing Crystal. She was not able to use it, for only a magician with great power could, but it was an almost indescribably beautiful object. It looked like a large spherical gem, but one in which a bright blue flame resided. She was enthralled by it. She wanted to touch it. To hold it. And one day, when Aldonaris was away, she acted on those impulses.

Tristaria snuck into the wizard's private chamber and after taking the All-seeing Crystal down from its stand, she held it in her little hands, excitedly marvelling at the magical light trapped inside it. But when she tried to put the All-seeing Crystal back, she dropped it onto the floor. Thankfully it did not break, but it did get a tiny crack. Horrified, Tristaria put the crystal back and left the room as quickly as she could.

For the next few days, she prayed and prayed that Aldoranis would not notice the crack, but of course, the old wizard eventually did. He gathered all his apprentices at the time, of which there were four, including Miralena and another, older boy named Olfalarin, and demanded to know who it was who had entered his private chamber without permission and damaged the All-seeing Crystal in the process. Tristaria was terrified, and although she was sure that her guilt was written all over her face, she kept quiet. The old wizard asked again, this time adding that until the culprit admitted their wrongdoing, none of them would get any dinner. By this point, Tristaria could no longer bear the tension. She began to raise her small, trembling hand. That was when Palantaros suddenly grabbed her wrist, and stopped her from raising her hand any further. Then he lifted his free hand and told Aldoranis that he was responsible for damaging the crystal. Despite herself, Tristaria breathed a sigh of relief.

As punishment, Palantaros was ordered to clean out the stables by himself for a whole week. Tristaria was too ashamed to speak to him for a while, but she eventually and thanked him for what he had done for her. Palantaros merely grinned and told her that it was no big deal, for she was his best friend.

Tears suddenly welled up in Tristaria's eyes, tears of guilt and shame, and Tristaria angrily wiped them away with her hands. "You miserable rat, Tristaria!" she admonished herself. "You were such a coward back then. Are you going to be one now?"

In answer to her question, Tristaria threw back her blanket and stood up from her bunk. Then she marched straight to the doorway of her room and went outside.

# TRISTARIA

*Unlike* earlier that night, Tristaria did not walk out in the open; instead she crept along the many shadows that filled the temple grounds, fearful of being spotted by anyone, even other novices. But fortunately her destination was the Storeroom, and it lay very near to the Novices' Quarters.

The Storeroom was a small, squat building made of stone. Apart from being used to keep the novices' belongings, it also held the tools the novices used to perform their allocated chores. This was where Tristaria had returned the broom she had used for sweeping earlier. It had a sturdy door, which was locked at night, but it also had a number of tall, narrow windows. It was a well-known fact among the novices that if you were small and thin enough, you could sneak into the storeroom through these slits. This suggested that the Storeroom had initially been built for another purpose, and was never meant to be a secure area.

In all her time at the temple, Tristaria had never attempted to enter the Storeroom through the windows, but since she was not tall and of slim build, she was confident she could. Standing side-on to one of the more secluded windows, she first of all put one leg through it, which was easy. Her upper body, however, was a challenge. It was a very tight squeeze, but in the end she was able to get her entire body through the window without too many scratches. After that, it was just a matter of pulling her other leg through.

Inside the Storeroom, it was quite dark. The narrow windows only allowed minimal light inside, so Tristaria had to pause for a few moments in order to give her eyes a bit of time to adjust. This also allowed her to get her bearings.

The Storeroom may not have been large, but it was completely filled with tall shelves arranged in tightly-spaced rows, rather like a library. However, instead of books, it contained an assortment of tools and other objects. Relying more on her fingertips and memory more than her eyes, Tristaria started moving along the shelves, searching for the one that held her personal belongings.

It was extremely quiet. The only sounds Tristaria could make out were her own nervous breathing, and the sound of her bare feet on the floor of the Storeroom. At one point, however, she heard a third noise: a low whine. Tristaria almost panicked, but the whine quickly faded away and she realized it was just the sound of a summer breeze finding its way through the windows.

After what seemed an eternity, Tristaria found her spot. It was a low shelf, close to the floor, so she squatted down beside it, and began rummaging through her things. She grabbed all the clothes in her possession: a simple white tunic, a dark blue cloak, a leather belt and leather sandals. These clothes were all more than two years old, and she had grown a fair bit in that time, so she knew they would feel uncomfortably small, but they were the only clothes she had and they would have to do.

Tristaria cautiously headed back the way she had come, and after carefully poking her head out of the window to make certain that no-one was in the vicinity, she tossed her clothes outside. Tristaria then exited the Storeroom by using the same method she had used to get in. However, by now her heart was racing and in her eagerness to get out, a thread from her nightdress snagged in the stone. "Drat," Tristaria muttered. She would need to repair the snag later.

After frantically gathering up her clothes from where they had landed on the ground, just under the window, Tristaria made a dash straight for the Novice's Quarters, no longer bothering to stick to the shadows.

Once she was back safely in her room, which was now lit only by faint moonlight, Tristaria wasted no time in slipping out of her nightdress and putting on all of her clothes, including her cloak. There was, of course, hardly any need for a cloak in the Kien Archipelago, even at night, but Tristaria reasoned that its deep blue colour would help conceal her in the dark.

After she finished dressing, Tristaria knelt beside her bunk and reached underneath it, into one of its corners. From there, she pulled out a small leather purse, which contained a small number of coins, mainly copper but some silver, that Tristaria had secretly stashed away, in case of an emergency. She put the purse under her belt, in a spot near the small of her back.

Now Tristaria was ready, except for one last thing. She went over to the corner of her room where her magic staff stood, leant up against the wall. It was quite an old staff; its amber crystal still shone brightly, but its wooden length was well-worn and covered with little marks and nicks and its golden metallic headpiece had long lost its lustre. For Tristaria, however, there was no more magnificent-looking artefact in the whole of Lianthia. This was because she had inherited it from a mage named Aliania.

Aliania was someone who had been very dear to Tristaria. Not only had she been the one who had raised Tristaria from a very young age, she had also been the one who had introduced her to Aldoranis. Furthermore, she had also been High Priestess of the Temple of Altaris for many years, and thus had inspired Tristaria to try and become a Priestess of Altaris herself.

Taking a firm hold of Aliania's staff, Tristaria immediately felt her heart fill with courage, and the nervousness she had felt earlier dissipated completely. Then, with a look of determination in her eyes, she turned and left her room.

# TRISTARIA

*There* was only one way in and out of the Temple of Altaris: the gates at the southern wall. During the day, these gates were almost always open, so that those who required healing could come and go freely. But now, in the middle of the night, it was shut tight. That meant that Tristaria would have to look for another way out.

Fortunately, Tristaria knew the layout of the temple extremely well. After all, she had been living in it for well over two years. On its north side, there was a line of broad oak trees, whose thick branches reached out over the temple wall and well beyond the temple grounds. That would be the easiest way out, Tristaria decided. The only other real option would be for her to use a ladder, but it would be difficult to get hold of one now. Furthermore, leaving behind such obvious evidence as a ladder would probably mean her departure would be discovered at first light. And that might possibly be enough time for someone from the temple to catch her before she could leave Kien Taril on the morning boat to Taraminas. Yes, it was much more preferable for her actions to remain undiscovered until at least the beginning of the morning prayers, which took place just before the morning classes.

Tristaria was confident that by now, almost everybody in the temple was asleep, so she took the most direct route to the northern wall. Upon reaching the trees, she carefully examined all of them before picking the one best suited to her purpose. Then, after standing her staff against it, she started climbing it.

Tristaria was quite good at climbing trees. She had climbed a lot of them with Palantaros. Indeed, that was one of the ways he would get them both into trouble: he would suddenly decide he wanted to go and pick fruit, instead of concentrating on the many chores that needed to be done.

Tristaria was soon atop a large bough, but she was not quite high enough to clear the wall. She needed to climb up higher. So she reached down for her staff and, with some difficulty, managed to stand it on the branch she herself was standing on. Then she pulled herself up onto a branch further up the tree. This one did extend over the wall, so after reaching down for her staff again, she began to walk carefully along it, using her staff to maintain her balance. Upon reaching the wall, she immediately stepped onto it. This caused her to momentarily lose her balance, but luckily she was able to regain it quickly.

Tristaria breathed a long sigh of relief and then cast a glance back at the temple grounds. This was it; after this, there would be no turning back.

Peering down into the gloomy woodlands beyond the wall, Tristaria spotted a nearby bush and she tossed her staff into it, Her staff landed right in the middle of the bush, with a soft rustle. Tristaria then began the process of getting back to the ground herself. First, she put herself in a sitting position on top of the wall, then she swivelled herself onto her belly, so that her legs were left dangling. The soles of her sandals were smooth and did not allow Tristaria to gain any sort of footing, so she let herself slide down the wall until she was hanging by her fingertips. She hung there for only an instant, before she let go. It was a big drop, but the grass along the wall was tall and lush, and it cushioned her fall somewhat. She landed on her feet, but her momentum sent her backwards, and she came to rest on her backside.

"Ow," Tristaria said, more out of habit than actual pain.

Getting back onto her feet, she dusted herself off and collected her staff from the bush. Then she set off along the undergrowth, following the wall until she had circled round to the gates and the dirt road in front of it,

This road led straight to the docks, where Tristaria could catch a boat to Taraminas. However, on the way to the docks, the road went through the village of Velsin, where a small guardhouse was located. The guardhouse provided protection for both Velsin and the Temple of Altaris, and Tristaria knew it was manned day and night, so she would be unable to go anywhere near it without being spotted. And if she was spotted, there was a chance she would be stopped and questioned. Tristaria desperately wanted to avoid such a scenario, so she decided to take a wide berth around Velsin. That meant travelling through the countryside, but she did not mind. The important thing was that she not miss the morning boat.

However, since Kien Taril was quite small, even with such a major detour it did not take very long for Tristaria to reach the docks. In fact, it was still quite dark when she came within sight of the pier and the handful of small buildings that surrounded it. So she found a secluded spot near the edge of the woodlands, in between a pair of large boulders, and lay down on the ground to get some sleep.

# TRISTARIA

*M*orning arrived and with it the sound of voices, which roused Tristaria from her slumber. She sat up and rubbed her eyes, gazing upwards as she did so; the sky above her was a clear pale blue.

Tristaria stood up and cautiously peaked over one of the boulders she had been lying next to, towards the road and the source of the sounds that had woken her. She saw that a wagon, pulled by a pair of oxen and carrying a number of commonfolk, was slowly trundling its way down towards the pier. The people on the wagon were talking loudly and laughing merrily.

After picking up her staff, Tristaria walked the short distance from the boulders to the road and began trailing after the wagon. Nobody seemed to notice her. Once the wagon reached the buildings near the water's edge, the passengers disembarked. Some of them went to mingle with a number of people who were already gathered at the docks, while others went to join the queue at the front of the boat owner's house, where an open window served as a sort of shop counter.

A few people glanced at Tristaria as she also joined the queue, probably because of her staff, but she did not think anybody would recognize her as a novice from the Temple of Altaris. Most likely they would assume she was a visitor to Kien Taril who was now going home.

When it was Tristaria's turn in front of the counter, the powerful-looking village woman standing behind it gave Tristaria a ferocious grin. "Where to, love?" she asked, in a good-natured way.

"Kien Sifel," Tristaria replied, almost meekly.

"Three silvies," the told woman told Tristaria, lifting up three fingers at the same time.

Tristaria took out three silver pieces from her purse and placed them on the counter. The woman scooped them up immediately and tossed them into a bowl on a table behind her. Then she grabbed a tin token from underneath the counter, with "KS" stamped onto it and handed it to Tristaria. "Give this to the boatman when you board," she instructed.

"Thank you," Tristaria responded. She was starting to move away from the counter, when she suddenly turned back. "Will the boat be leaving soon?" she asked.

"Very soon, love," the woman said.

Tristaria left the counter and made her way down to the pier, where three sailing vessels were moored, one large and two small. The large boat was already full, while the other two were as yet empty.

"Anybody else for Kerastes?" the burly boatman on the large boat shouted from atop the gangplank that connected the vessel to the pier. He glanced at Tristaria, and she gave him an exaggerated shake of her head, to make it clear to him she was not going to Port Kerastes. The boatman then raised the gangplank and went to the helm, while a colleague removed the mooring ropes. A few moments later, the large vessel was on its way and Tristaria watched it for a long while as it sailed straight towards the southern horizon. She found herself thinking of Eramaklis, and she wondered if he was already in Kerastes.

Turning her attention away from the sea, Tristaria looked at the two remaining boats. There was still no sign of any movement on either of them, so she went over to one of the pier's bollards and sat down on it, facing back towards the hills. From this point, the road to Velsin was plainly visible, and if anyone was going to come from the temple looking for her, they would come down that very road, so Tristaria wanted a clear view of it. Of course, she was not exactly sure what she would do in the event someone did come looking for her. There wasn't much point in trying to flee, because she had nowhere to flee to.

Other wagons came down the hill, as well as many people on foot, but amongst them there was nobody Tristaria recognized. After a while, Tristaria relaxed. Then she began to get a little bit bored. She stared down at her feet and noticed her toes were jutting out from the soles of her old battered sandals quite at bit. She wished she could get a new pair, but of course she could not afford to.

"Kien Sifel!" someone shouted. Tristaria looked up at the boats and on the nearest of them, a boatman had appeared, seemingly out of nowhere. He had just lowered the gangplank and was beckoning towards those onshore to come forward.

Tristaria stood up in a flash and hurried to the boat, eager to be the first to board. She crossed the gangplank and handed the wiry old boatman her token. "Thank you, young lady," he said, winking at her. "Hope you have a pleasant voyage."

Tristaria went straight to the bow of the small boat and then turned around to watch as the other passengers slowly made their way down the pier and onto the deck. They took an awfully long time about it, and Tristaria was soon wishing that they would all hurry up. She kept glancing up at the hills, fearing that any moment someone from the temple would come running down the road, screaming for the boat not to leave. But thankfully this did not happen. The passengers finished boarding and the boatman raised the gangplank, loosened the mooring rope and stepped up to the helm. Then the boat began to move.

Section 7

# TRISTARIA

*Despite* its relative proximity to Kien Taril, Tristaria had never seen the town of Taraminas, and she was somewhat excited to see what it looked like. So later that day, when the boat pulled up to a dock that was not much bigger than the one on Kien Taril, she was surprised, as well as a little concerned.

"This can't be Taraminas" she told herself aloud, as the passengers started disembarking.

Someone near her laughed. "No, young mage, this isn't Taraminas!" a plump, cheerful-looking man standing nearby informed her. "This is just a small dock for the boats coming from the north. Taraminas is on the other side of the island."

"Oh, I see," Tristaria said, suddenly wishing that she had had time to plan her journey better. She had assumed the boat would take her straight to Taraminas, but now it looked as though she would need to cover the remaining distance on foot.

Once Tristaria stepped off the boat, she drifted with most of the other passengers from the pier to a small collection of buildings nearby, which were not unlike the ones on Kien Taril. Quite a lot of people were about, some on foot and some in wagons. As far as Tristaria could tell, they were either passengers waiting to catch the boat back to Kien Taril, or they were waiting to meet someone who had just come from there.

Those in the latter group began to disperse along two different roads: one which climbed into the hills, and another which wound its way around the ragged shore. Tristaria was deliberating which one was more likely to lead to Taraminas, when she heard someone call out behind her. "Young mage!" the voice said.

Tristaria immediately recognized the voice as that of the man who had spoken to her briefly on the boat, only a few moments earlier. She looked behind her and sure enough, the same plump man was waving at her. He was sitting at the front of a small horse-drawn cart, next to an equally plump woman. The man beckoned Tristaria to come closer, so she went over to his cart.

"You're headed for Taraminas, right?" the man asked.

Tristaria nodded.

"Well, we're headed to the western valley, so we can take you part of the way there," he explained. "You'll have to sit in the back with Olin, though." Only then did Tristaria notice there was a large piglet lying in the back of the cart.

Tristaria shrugged. "I don't mind, as long as Olin doesn't," she said.

The man chuckled. "Oh, Olin won't mind, will ya girl?" He reached back to give Olin a quick scratch. "She's a friendly piggy, she is." Olin gave a snort, seemingly in acknowledgement. "Hop on the back then, young mage."

Tristaria climbed onto the cart and sat down in a corner, so that both her legs were left dangling freely. Olin was not that big, but neither was the cart, and as friendly as Olin might be, Tristaria did not wish to intrude upon her personal space.

Tristaria smiled at the piglet. "Hello," she said.

Olin lifted her head up and looked at Tristaria inquisitively, but this time the piglet made no sound. She only blinked a few times, then lay her head down once more.

"All right, then. Let's get going, shall we?" The man pulled on the reins and the horse and cart began to move up the road, into the hills. "My name is Dolsor, by the way," the man ventured. "And this is my dear wife, Balanis."

"Nice to meet you. I'm Tristaria,"

"Nice to meet you too, Tristaria," Balanis said.

The road soon reached the top of the hills, where it levelled out and entered wooded land. At this point, Dolsor began to tell Tristaria about himself and his wife. They were pig farmers, but they were soon going to retire and move to a more secluded area. That was why Dolsor had gone to Kien Taril: he knew someone who lived there, and he went to visit them in order to find out their opinion of Velsin.

"Are you from Velsin, Tristaria?" Dolsor asked after a while. "Or somewhere else?"

"Somewhere else," Tristaria answered.

"So you're a traveller, then?"

"At the moment, yes." So far so good, Tristaria thought to herself. She had not yet resorted to lies.

"And why are you headed for Taraminas?" Balanis enquired.

Now things were going to get tricky. "I... I seek an audience with King Galasius."

"King Galasius?" Dolsor and Balanis said, in unison.

"Must be something really important, I gather" Dolsor remarked.

"Yes, it is," Tristaria said. "For me, at least."

As the cart slowly made the long journey southwards, the sun dipped lower and lower in the sky, until the shadows from the woods had more or less stretched across the road. Eventually, however, they reached a three-way junction and here, Dolsor pulled on the reins, bringing the cart to a halt.

"Here we are, Tristaria," Dolsor said. "This is as far as we can take you."

Tristaria jumped off the cart. "Thank you kindly for the ride."

"Our pleasure," Dolsor said. "Farewell, young mage, and take care of yourself!"

"I will," Tristaria responded, as the cart began to move down the road to the right. "Farewell Dolsor! Farewell Balanis! And farewell Olin!"

The cart was soon out of sight and Tristaria turned her attention to the road on the left. In the distance, she could just make out smoke rising above the woods; she was very close to Taraminas now.

# TRISTARIA

*It* was dusk when Tristaria reached the stockade that protected the landward side of the port town of Taraminas. There were several guards at the gates, but they paid little heed to her as she went past them, and into the town.

As she walked along a long broad street, flanked on either side by large buildings, Tristaria noted there were people still about, despite the fact it was late in the day. However, quite a number of these people seemed to be drunk: one person threw up right in front of where Tristaria was walking, forcing her to take a wide berth around the mess left on the cobblestones.

At the end of the street, there was a small square, with a tall fountain at its centre. The fountain depicted a tall beautiful woman wrestling a mighty shark.

Tristaria had read a little bit about this woman: she was the Protectress of Taraminas. Legend told that many, many years ago, when the great warrior Algis tried to land on Kien Sifel, a monstrous shark had attacked his ship and sunk it. This terrible beast then tried to devour Algis, but luckily a goddess of the sea took pity on the warrior. She fought and killed the shark, saving Algis' life. Subsequently, the grateful warrior founded Taraminas in the goddess' honour, and became the town's first king.

There were several people in the vicinity of the fountain. Most of them were strolling about, in pairs or small groups, but a large group had gathered around a musician, who was playing a lute. On the ground, at the musician's feet, sat a small wooden bowl and, as Tristaria looked on, someone dropped a coin into it.

Drawn by the pleasant sound of the lute, Tristaria began wandering absentmindedly towards the musician, but then she abruptly stopped and sniffed the air.

The smell that had caught Tristaria's attention emanated from the far side of the fountain, where a young townswoman with a food stall was selling cooked potatoes. Realizing how hungry she now was, Tristaria changed course and went straight over to the food stall.

"How much are the potatoes?" she asked the woman.

"Normally you get two for a copper piece," the woman replied. "But I'm done for today, so I'll let you have three for that price."

Tristaria handed over a coin without giving it a second thought, her mouth already watering. The potatoes were very hot, so she used her cloak to receive them, then she went over to sit at the fountain, facing the musician.

As she quietly ate her potatoes, Tristaria listened to the music, but she also took the chance to examine her surroundings. Four streets met at the fountain square, including the one that she had just traversed. Of the remaining three, one ended up disappearing into nondescript houses, one led to an impressive looking temple, most likely dedicated to the Protectress, and one led to what looked like a second, larger square. She decided the larger square was where King Galasius' abode was most likely to be. And even if it was not, the larger square would provide her with a better view of the town.

After she finished eating, Tristaria looked up at the sky. It was a sombre grey colour now, as the sun had set, but in the sun's place a half moon shone brightly and the stars were beginning to appear. There was not much of a chance she would be able to meet King Galasius this late in the day, but she at least wanted to find out exactly where he lived.

The lute player soon finished playing and the crowd cheered. Tristaria also clapped, having enjoyed the music. The musician then bowed theatrically and said a few words to those gathered about him. Like the woman in the food stall, it looked as though he was also done for the day and many onlookers happily tossed coins into his bowl. Tristaria wished she had more money, so she could give the lute player a coin too, but of course, she had to be careful with the little money she had, especially since she would most definitely need to pay for lodging that night.

Tristaria left the fountain and headed up the street that led to the big square. Halfway there, a tall scruffy youth came hurriedly out of an alleyway and ran straight into her, knocking her to the ground and making her drop her staff. The youth fell down too, but he was quickly back on his feet, with a worried expression on his face.

"Oh, I'm terribly sorry!" The youth said. "Are you all right, miss?"

Tristaria was a little dazed, but she had not been injured. "I'm... I'm fine. Just a little—"

"Here, let me help you up," the youth said. He took Tristaria by the hand, and gently pulled her to her feet. "No cuts?" he asked, looking her over.

"No, no. I'm fine."

"Oh, but look! I've gotten your lovely cloak all dirty. Let me clean it for you."

"No, you don't need to do that."

The youth ignored Tristaria and proceeded to brush the dirt off her cloak, even though it did not seem that dirty to Tristaria's eyes. The youth then picked up Tristaria's staff from the ground and handed it to her.

"Thank you," Tristaria said.

The youth smiled. "You have a good evening, miss."

With that, the youth ran off towards the fountain. Tristaria watched him go until he was out of sight. "I wonder why he was in such a hurry?" she wondered, frowning. Then she continued on her way.

# TRISTARIA

*There* was no mistaking the king's abode: it was a large, imposing stone keep surrounded by a tall stone wall that completely dominated one side of the large square. And although it was now dark, the keep's main gates were easy to see: they were well-illuminated by a pair of torches on the wall, one on either side of the gates. These torches also illuminated two soldiers who guarded the gates. Wearing a shield and a helmet and armed with a spear and a short sword, the soldiers cast long flickering shadows on the cobblestones.

As Tristaria drew close to the gates, which were shut, the soldier who stood closest to her looked her way. "On your way, miss," the soldier said. "No loitering allowed around here at this time of day."

Not wanting to appear threatening, Tristaria came to a complete halt some distance from the gates. "I was hoping to speak to the king..." she explained.

The guard looked amused, "Sure you were, but no-one can speak to him this late. Come back tomorrow."

Tristaria took a step back. "Wh–what time should I come?"

"Any time you bloody well like," the guard snapped, making Tristaria jump. "As long as it's during the day and not my bloody shift again."

A wide-eyed Tristaria nodded quickly and walked away without saying another word. Only when she was well away from the gates, did she dare look back at them. "That soldier didn't need to be so rude," she said to herself.

Tristaria made her way to the centre of the square, where a giant statue of Algis, the founding king of Taraminas stood. The statue was surrounded by several stalls, but none of them were open. In fact, their owners were all in the process of packing up for the day. Tristaria decided it was time for her to look for a place to stay the night.

Fortunately, there was an inn right across from the keep, with the signboard hanging over its doorway proclaiming it to be "The King's Pride". However, judging by the sign's well-worn appearance, Tristaria doubted there was any truth in this name.

The front room of the inn was empty, apart from the innkeeper, of course. He was a large, bearded man, and he was sitting behind a counter in a comfortable chair, looking half-asleep. But when he noticed Tristaria, he immediately became alert and hurriedly got to his feet.

"I take it you are looking for a room, young lady?" the innkeeper asked, almost gleefully.

"Yes... But how much are they?"

"I'm afraid all our finest rooms have been taken, But I do have a couple in the basement at a bargain price of five silver pieces."

"Five silver pieces?" Tristaria repeated, incredulously.

"Yes, hard to believe, isn't it?" the innkeeper said, misreading Tristaria's reaction completely.

Tristaria thought for a bit. The cost for a room was more than she had anticipated, but it was probably unwise to go looking for another inn at this time of night. Even if she did find another one, there was no guarantee that the rooms would be any cheaper, or that it would even have vacancies.

"All right, I'll take a room."

The innkeeper said nothing, but held out a hand.

Tristaria reached behind her back... And that was when she realized her purse was no longer there. "My purse, it's gone!" she exclaimed.

The innkeeper's expression turned sour, and he rolled his eyes. "Oh dear, not again. How many times have I heard that this week alone?"

Tristaria found herself getting angry. "But it's true! I had it just a moment ago." She looked about desperately on the floor around her. "I must have dropped it somewhere."

"Yes, I bet you did. Now go and try your little act on someone else, because it's not going to work on me." The innkeeper then sat back down again, paying no more attention to Tristaria.

Her purse was not in the inn, so Tristaria went back outside. It was not there either. Where could she have dropped it? She had had it when she paid for the potatoes, so... Then the answer came to her. The youth! The youth who had run into her! She realized that he must have somehow stolen her purse while he pretended to clean her cloak.

Tristaria felt like crying. She raised her eyes to the night sky and blinked rapidly, in an effort to stop her tears from materializing. As she was doing this, she heard a soft meow from nearby, apparently from the direction of the inn.

Tristaria turned her head and heard the sound again, this time a bit louder. Now she could tell it was not actually coming from the inn itself, but from a narrow gap between the inn and the building beside it, where a wild, unkempt bush had taken up residence.

Walking over to the bush, Tristaria spotted a pair of luminous eyes in the darkness behind it. They were the eyes of a cat and they were staring right back at her.

"Hello," Tristaria said to the cat. "Is this your home?"

The cat continued looking at Tristaria, but made no sound.

"Would it be all right if I stay here tonight? I promise I won't be any trouble."

The cat tilted its head slightly and then meowed softly. Tristaria took this as a yes.

The bush was full of thorns, so Tristaria used her cloak to protect herself as she squeezed past it, to the spot where the cat was sitting. The cat was not at all frightened by her approach and it did not move away. After standing her staff up against the wall, Tristaria spread her cloak out on the ground, then lay down on it, curling herself into a ball.

"I'm afraid today hasn't been the best of days," Tristaria said to the cat, sadly. "But hopefully tomorrow will be better." The cat said nothing, but it ambled onto Tristaria's cloak, and just like Tristaria, it lay down on it in a tight ball. Tristaria smiled. In a matter of moments, they were both fast asleep.

The next morning, when Tristaria awoke to the noise of various activities in the main square, the cat had gone. "I didn't even have the chance to say thank you," Tristaria said, regretfully, as she rubbed the sleepiness from her eyes.

Tristaria stood up and peered over the thorny bush, towards the square. The sun had just begun to climb the sky, but there were already a lot of people about. Tristaria picked up her cloak and staff. Then, as she had done on the previous night, she used her cloak to protect herself from the bush as she made her way back into the square. A few passers-by glanced briefly at her as she emerged from the shadow of the inn, but no-one seemed surprised. Tristaria sighed. Based on her appearance, she was sure they all assumed she was just a vagabond.

Putting on her cloak, Tristaria began crossing the square in the direction of the king's keep, and as she carefully weaved through the crowds she had a good look around her. There were so many things going on: there was a troupe of acrobats, their faces painted in bright colours, performing great leaps and tumbles; there was a puppeteer, performing for a group of children; and there was even another musician, this one accompanied by a lovely female singer. But the thing that caught Tristaria's attention the most were the numerous food stalls, which she had walked past the day before. Now, however, they were full of activity and the pleasant odours of various treats filled the air. But since she had no money, Tristaria did her best to ignore these odours and she continued on to the king's keep.

As was the case the night before, the gates were shut and guarded by a pair of soldiers and these soldiers were talking to a tall, thin man, who was standing near a large cart, drawn by two horses. Judging by his fine clothes and extravagant jewellery, Tristaria guessed the man was a merchant. Indeed, his cart was laden with what looked like giant rolls of dyed cloth. He seemed somewhat agitated, so Tristaria casually strolled towards the gates at an angle, allowing her to discreetly eavesdrop on what was being said.

"And what time did he go to the temple?" the man was asking the guards.

"Only a short time ago," one of the soldiers responded. "So we don't expect he'll be back anytime soon."

"But the king promised me an audience today!"

"Why don't you come back in the afternoon?" the second soldier suggested. "That's still today, right?"

"No, that's impossible. I'm due to board a ship for Akeminos this afternoon."

"Well, then we can't help you, I'm afraid."

The merchant continued arguing with the guards, but Tristaria had heard enough. King Galasius was not in his keep; he had gone to the temple and Tristaria had a feeling it was the temple she had seen the day before.

Hurrying away from the keep, Tristaria headed for the fountain square. On the way there, she passed the spot at which she had had that unfortunate encounter with the youth and she had a quick, nervous glance down the narrow alleyway he had emerged from. But the alleyway was well-lit now and there was no-one lurking in it.

Like the main square, the fountain square was also full of people, forcing Tristaria to slow down as she passed through it. But once she was out of it, and into the street that led up to the temple, she was able to quicken her pace once more.

As Tristaria got closer to the temple, which sat at a three-way junction, she was able to discern its appearance more clearly. It was a grey-coloured structure, made from granite, and it had been decorated with a number of beautiful reliefs depicting the legend of the Protectress of Taraminas. It was not a particularly large structure, although it certainly dwarfed the buildings in its vicinity, but it had a towering spire on its roof, one which seemed to stretch all the way to the sky.

The main entrance to the temple was at the top of a series of steps, curved in design, and at the base of these steps, a large raucous group of people had gathered. It looked as though these people wanted to enter the temple, but they were being prevented from doing so by no less than six of the towns' soldiers.

"Listen to me, will you?" one of the soldiers, who seemed to be in charge, was saying. "The temple is off limits to the public right now. King Galasius is holding a private service here with his personal mages."

A number of people raised their voices in protest, but the soldier dismissed them with a wave of his hand.

"Don't start with me," the soldier said. "None of you lot are getting in until the king's private service is over. Now, make way for the king's mages."

Tristaria, who was now standing somewhere at the back of the crowd, turned to see a group of six men and women approaching. They were all carrying staffs and they were all dressed head-to-toe in deep blue robes with hoods. The crowd dutifully parted to make a path for them as they started up the steps.

Tristaria suddenly saw her chance to get inside the temple. She fell into step at the rear of the line of mages, pulling on the hood of her cloak as she did so. She sort of looked the part: she had a staff, of course, and her cloak was of a similar colour to the robes the mages wore, although hers barely covered her legs. But fortune was with her today; the soldiers, who were all keeping their eyes on the crowd, did not even glance at her, allowing her to enter the temple completely unchallenged.

# TRISTARIA

$\mathcal{T}$*he* main chamber of the Temple of the Protectress was like the ones in most temples in Lianthia. It was a large, circular room with a dais in the centre, where a statue of the Protectress stood. Around the dais were dozens of wooden benches which had been arranged into six sections, separated by six aisles. In all, the benches could probably seat hundreds of people, but they were all now empty, except for one bench right in front of the dais. There, a group of four people were sitting.

The mages slowly filed up one of the aisles and as they made their way towards the dais, they cut across several shafts of light that emanated from the chamber's eastward-facing windows. Tristaria continued following this solemn procession until it was about halfway up the aisle, then she finally lost her nerve and she hastily sat down on the bench nearest to her.

The mages went straight over to the group sitting at the front, bowing low as they did. The group, in turn, stood up to acknowledge the mages. Out of the four individuals in the group, the two that stood out were the two in the middle; one was a large, broad-shouldered man and the other was a somewhat rotund woman. Both were dressed in fine clothes, so they were without a doubt King Galasius and his wife. The remaining two people, a man and a woman, wore simple clothes, so they were most likely servants.

After King Galasius and his companions sat back down, the mages stepped onto the dais and formed a circle around the statue of the Protectress. Then they raised their arms and faces in unison, and a hypnotic chant began to echo around the temple.

The mage's ceremony, as far as Tristaria could gather, was being conducted for an individual who was ill, took quite a while, and by the time it was over, the shafts of light in the chamber had shortened into nothingness. The mages then descended from the dais and once more approached the king and his companions. The two groups spoke briefly this time, then they started to walk out of the chamber together, with the king taking the lead.

Seeing the king approaching her filled Tristaria with sudden trepidation and she did not have the nerve to raise her voice to get his attention. But in the end, she didn't need to; the king spotted her and came to a halt. His wife and servants did the same, all of them looking a bit startled, but the mages kept walking.

King Galasius frowned at Tristaria. "What are you doing here?" he demanded. "Why weren't you with the others on the dais?"

Tristaria quickly got to her feet and, after removing her hood, bowed low to the king. She opened her mouth to reply, but the king spoke again before she could say anything.

"Wait a moment, you're not one of my mages. Who are you?"

"My name is Tristaria, your highness. And you are correct. I am not one of your mages. I am a novice from the Temple of Altaris and—"

"Altaris? You mean the one on Kien Taril?"

"Yes, your Highness."

The king looked confused. "So why are you here? And how did you get past the guards?"

"I'm sorry for coming in here during your private ceremony, I meant no disrespect, but there was an urgent matter I—"

"Don't talk to me about urgent matters, child," Galasius said, cutting Tristaria off. "I have plenty of those to deal with as it is."

The king then walked off towards the exit and although both his servants followed him, the queen did not. She looked at Tristaria curiously. "If you are from the Temple of Altaris, you must know about healing." she said in a gentle voice. "Is that correct?"

"Yes, your highness," Tristaria replied.

"Come, Esilias," Galasius called out to his wife. "We must go!"

"Galasius, did you not hear her? She said she knows about healing!"

"Yes, I heard."

"Perhaps she can help Losurion."

The king returned to where his wife stood, looking unimpressed.

"Esilias, she's only a novice," he said. "A beginner. Best to leave the matter to our own mages."

"But they are just scholars, not dedicated healers," the queen rejoined. Then, before the king could get another word in, she spoke to Tristaria again. "What was it that you wanted to talk to my husband about, dear?"

"My friend Palantaros."

"Palantaros?" the queen repeated. "The boy who set fire to the orchards?"

"I'm sure it wasn't intentional," Tristaria said quickly.

"Even if it wasn't, the little fool caused a lot of damage," the king growled. But then he raised his eyebrows. "Wait a moment. Did you say he is your friend? Are you here to pay his fine?"

Tristaria shook her head. "Unfortunately I don't have that amount of money. I was hoping you would be able to show Palantaros some mercy because—"

"Well then you're just wasting our time," Galasius said and promptly walked off once more. "Let's go, Esilias!"

There was a look of disappointment on the queen's face as she took a few paces down the aisle, but she suddenly turned and faced Tristaria once again.

"Please, I beg you, come to the rear gate of the keep as soon as you can," she whispered. "There will be a girl waiting there for you. Just tell her that you're the healer and she'll let you in. I wish to speak to you in private."

Esilias then hurried outside, leaving Tristaria standing in the middle of the aisle, slightly confused. But when the people who had been waiting outside slowly began to drift into the chamber, she too hurried outside.

Section 12

# TRISTARIA

*Although* she was not exactly sure what it was the queen wanted to talk to her about, Tristaria decided to do as the queen had asked, if only for the fact that doing so might give her another chance to try and help Palantaros. There was a slight problem, however, and that was that she did not know how to get to the rear gate of the king's keep. So Tristaria rushed back to the main square of Taraminas, with the intention of asking the soldiers at the front gates of the keep for directions. But once she got there, she found herself faced with another slight problem.

Quite a long queue had built up in front of the king's keep during the day, and although the front gates were now wide open, the queue was moving incredibly slowly. Unsurprisingly, the people in line looked hot and tired and tempers were short. Several people could be heard shouting at the soldiers, most of who were either pleading or demanding to be let in as quickly as possible. Tristaria decided it was best to avoid this commotion entirely and instead began looking for a way to circle round the keep.

To one side of the keep, there was what looked like a rather busy artisans' market; to the other there was a narrow strip of undisturbed woods. Worried about wasting too much time in a crowd, Tristaria darted into the woods and nimbly began avoiding tree trunks and shrubs as she raced along the keep's wall.

However, upon reaching the end of the woods, near the rear corner of the keep, Tristaria was forced to come to a complete halt; a canal that ran parallel to the keep's rear wall barred her way forward. The canal was not especially wide, but it looked quite deep and the water in it was running rapidly. Hoping there might be a better spot to cross the canal nearby, Tristaria walked away from the keep for a little while, but if anything, the canal seemed to get wider in this direction, so she decided to throw caution to the wind.

After backing up a little, Tristaria ran as fast as she could towards the canal and jumped. Her leading foot easily cleared it, but her trailing foot clipped the top of the canal's bank. As a result, she fell to the ground and rolled over a couple of times, finally coming to rest in the middle of a pile of fallen leaves. But Tristaria instantly got back on her feet and began following the canal along the keep's rear wall.

Before long, the canal was joined by a narrow stone path and this path led Tristaria through a group of small buildings. Judging by the smell of manure, she guessed that these buildings were stables, but she did not pay much attention to them; her eyes were fixed on the wall.

By now, Tristaria was tiring and perspiring profusely. She was also starting to worry that she had somehow missed the rear gate and that she was going to end up back at the main square. But then she saw it: a small wooden door in the wall up ahead. The door was ajar and the face of a young girl was peering expectantly around it.

"I'm the healer," Tristaria said to the girl, breathlessly.

The girl smiled and nodded. "Come inside," she said, beckoning to Tristaria as she spoke.

Naturally, in order to get to the gate, Tristaria had to once again cross the canal. However, in front of the gate there were a series of sturdy-looking wooden posts which had been driven into the bottom of the canal precisely for this purpose. So thankfully, there was no need for her to jump this time.

Once Tristaria was safely across the canal and inside the keep, the girl bolted the door shut. "Please follow me," the girl said, and then she led Tristaria up a little gravel path that wound its way through a small garden, full of brightly-coloured flowers. The path came to an end right before a door at the back of the keep. However, the girl ignored this door, and instead went round the keep, where there was a large paved area decorated with several statues and a small fountain.

When they reached the fountain, the girl turned to Tristaria. "Please wait here while I go and inform Queen Esilias that you have arrived," the girl said. Then she disappeared into the keep through a small side-door that lay close by.

Left alone for a moment, Tristaria took the opportunity to check her appearance in the water of the fountain. She looked awful. She was covered in perspiration and the tumble she had taken earlier had left her covered head to toe with dirt, leaves and small twigs, not to mention several little scratches. Tristaria did her best to brush away the more obvious bits of debris from her body, and she had more or less succeeded in doing this when the queen suddenly appeared, with the young girl from before at her side.

Esilias looked elated. "Thank the Protectress you came!" she exclaimed, before giving Tristaria a brief embrace. "Tell me, child, what is your name?"

"Tristaria, your highness."

"Tristaria," the queen repeated. "You may call me Esilias, if you wish. Now, The reason I asked you here, Tristaria, is because I want to ask you for your help. You see, three days ago, while Losurion, my youngest son, was playing in the woods next to the keep, he was bitten by an asp. Our mages have tried their best to heal him, but alas they have so far been unable to do so. And that's no surprise, I must say. You see, none of them have been specifically trained in healing. Not like you."

"So you want me to try to heal your son?" Tristaria asked, even though she knew what the answer would be.

"Yes!"

"But... I'm only a novice..."

"Oh, don't worry about what my husband said at the temple. Unlike me, he does not realize that it is the will of the Protectress that brought you here. She has answered our prayers by sending you to us."

"But..."

"Please, Tristaria," the queen implored, with a grave expression on her face. "I fear my son's will to live is steadily ebbing away and if I was to lose him..."

Tristaria bit her lip. For her own safety, she was not supposed to perform any sort of healing without supervision from a senior priestess. But how could she refuse the earnest plea of a mother in great need?

"Very well," Tristaria said. "I will try,"

# TRISTARIA

*U*pon entering Prince Losurion's chamber, in the company of the queen and the young girl who had let her into the keep, Tristaria found herself in a room that was truly fit for a prince. It was spacious and beautifully decorated but since all the windows in it had been tightly shuttered, it was also quite gloomy and stuffy. The prince himself was in the centre of the room, lying unconscious on a large feather bed. Apart from a loincloth he was naked, although he did have a small bandage on one forearm where, Tristaria presumed, the asp had struck him. Next to the prince's bed, there was a small table with a basin of water on it where a woman, ostensibly another servant, was busily wringing a wet cloth. After briefly looking to see who had entered the room, the woman proceeded to gently dab the cloth on the prince's brow.

Even from where she stood, which was several paces away from the bed, it was immediately obvious to Tristaria that Losurion was feverish: his cheeks were flushed and there were beads of sweat all over his body. Curing the prince would undoubtedly be an enormously taxing exercise, but even so, Tristaria was determined to do her best.

Tristaria turned to Esilias. "I will need the windows to be open," she said.

The queen only needed to glance at the girl beside her, and the girl went at once to open all the shutters. The room brightened up significantly and as fresh air entered the room, the stuffiness started to dissipate, but this was not the reason Tristaria had wanted the windows open. She was a novice from the Temple of Altaris, the Sun Goddess, and thus sunlight was a great asset to her. That is not to say she was unable to use magic without it; after all, like any other magic-user, her magical energy came from deep within herself. However, with sunlight, her power was greatly enhanced.

After removing her cloak and putting it aside, Tristaria sat down, cross-legged, in the middle of one of the many sunlit spots that now covered the floor. Then she placed her staff across her thighs and looked over at the expectant face of the queen. "I'm afraid I will need a bit of time," Tristaria said. A very powerful healer, such as High Priestess Lusianis, could have cured the prince in a heartbeat. But Tristaria was still a young girl and a novice. Something like that was well beyond her.

"I understand," Esilias said in response.

With hands clasped together firmly and her eyes shut tight, Tristaria lifted her face towards the sun, and then in a quiet voice she began to chant. "Lady Altaris, giver of light, please help your humble servant make this ill right," she said, over and over again. It was the most basic of incantations, but it allowed her to accumulate magical energy into her staff, or to be more specific, the power crystal in her staff. At first, nothing seemed to happen. But after some time had passed, the crystal began to glow, faintly at first, but soon it was bright enough to fill the entire room with a soft, yellow glow. By this time, Tristaria was perspiring freely once again, and her perspiration fell in drips to the floor, but the floor had gotten quite hot and so the drips evaporated almost immediately.

When Tristaria was satisfied that she had accumulated enough energy, she stopped chanting and started taking long deep breaths. She needed to recuperate at least a small fraction of her energy, so that she could focus the power in the staff properly and thus use it without being wasteful. Tristaria took one last long breath and then she opened her eyes, She was ready.

Tristaria stood up and walked to the bed, where she turned to face Esilias, whose look of expectancy had increased visibly. "I will now attempt to drive the poison from the prince's body and heal his wound," Tristaria declared. In response to this, the woman with the cloth stepped away from the bed, but the queen moved closer to it.

Tristaria then turned to Losurion and, with a look of determination in her eyes, she held her staff over the prince's injury and drew several more deep breaths. "Oh tainted blood and sundered flesh, begone!" she cried. Instantly, there was a blinding flash from her power crystal, and everyone, except for Tristaria, was forced to look away. However, Tristaria did stumble backwards slightly, as if she had received a sharp but invisible blow to her body.

As the afterglow of the flash slowly faded and vanished, Tristaria lowered her staff and let out a long, tired sigh.

"Is it done?" Esilias asked.

Tristaria wiped the perspiration from her brow. "Yes, you can remove his bandage now."

The queen did not need any further prompting; she immediately tore the cloth strip from her son's arm, and lo! There was not a single mark to be seen on the skin beneath it.

Esilias gasped, as though she could not believe her eyes. She looked up at Tristaria and was about to say something, when her son stirred. He opened his eyes, and he looked straight up at the queen. "Mama...?" the prince said, dreamily.

Upon hearing this, Esilias pulled him up from the bed towards her and embraced him. "Oh my treasure, I was so worried about you!" she cried and tears of joy started streaming down her face. Around her, the servants also started shedding tears.

Tristaria suddenly felt a little awkward, as if she was intruding on a private affair, but nevertheless she too was moved by the touching scene before her. So much so, in fact, that a little tear appeared in her eye, but she quickly brushed it away. And that was when her head started to spin. Tristaria lost her balance and dropped her staff, which fell to the floor with a loud clatter, and this caused everyone in the room, except for the prince, to look in her direction.

"Tristaria!" the queen exclaimed. "What's wrong?"

"N—nothing, your highness, I'm just—" Tristaria began to say, then she collapsed.

# TRISTARIA

*W*hen Tristaria regained consciousness, she found herself on top of a large comfortable feather bed, with a light blanket covering most of her body. The bed was very much like the one the prince had been lying on, but she was in a different room; this room was smaller than the prince's room and largely devoid of furniture. This suggested that it was a room reserved for guests and not one that was normally in use.

"Oh good," Tristaria heard a voice say. "You're finally awake!"

Turning her head towards the source of the voice, Tristaria saw that it had come from a young woman, yet another servant, who was sitting on a chair next to the bed.

The woman smiled at Tristaria. "The queen was very worried about you, miss," she said. "I'd better go and tell her that you've come to, right away!" And with that, the woman stood up and left the room.

After being alone for a while, Tristaria suddenly remembered her staff and she sat up with a jolt, looking all around the room for it. But to her relief her staff was right beside her, carefully propped up against the bedhead.

Feeling relieved, Tristaria lay back down and her gaze soon fell upon one of several windows in the room. Outside, the colour of the sky was dull and subdued. She wondered how long she had slept for. All afternoon? Or possibly all night as well? She couldn't be sure. She had never attempted to use such powerful magic in her life before, so she was unsure how much time was needed to recover.

Tristaria's thoughts then turned to what had happened in the prince's room earlier. On reflection, she had done a very risky thing and she could already picture the high priestess chastising her for her recklessness.

Of course, there had never been any danger to the young prince; if Tristaria's magic had failed, he would have simply been left unhealed. The only one in danger had been Tristaria herself. She had asked her body to endure an ordeal that it was not yet fully prepared for. It could have killed her, but as far as she could tell, she seemed to have gotten through this ordeal unscathed, although only time would tell if she had suffered any permanent damage. Regardless of any repercussions, however, Tristaria had no regrets over what she had done; she was certain any healer in her situation would have done the same.

No longer content to remain lying in bed, Tristaria pulled the blanket away from her body and placed her bare feet on the floor. Then, with a little bit of effort, she got up and walked over to the nearest window, where she was greeted by a gentle breeze. It was a very pleasant sensation, which made her feel reinvigorated.

Looking outside, Tristaria saw that the room she was in was on the second level of the keep, so not only could she see a large part of Taraminas, she could also see the sea beyond. And despite the weak light, she could even make out large vessels on the horizon, as they made their way to and from Lianthia.

Tristaria was about to turn away from the window, when she spotted a small copse of trees only a short distance away, within the grounds of the king's keep. She quickly realized this was the king's orchard. Or, to be more precise, what remained of it.

Near the middle of the orchard, there was a large black mark on the ground, as if a fireball had landed there. The trees in the immediate vicinity of this mark had been all but obliterated, and although those further away were still standing, they all appeared to have suffered damage to some degree. Not surprisingly, there were no apples to be seen anywhere.

Tristaria sighed. She now understood King Galasius' great anger at Palantaros, but she was still hopeful that at the very least she would be given a chance to plead Palantaros' case anew, especially after her efforts to help Prince Losurion.

At that moment, Queen Esilias entered the room, along with her servant. Esilias approached Tristaria, a warm smile on her face. "It's good to see you on your feet again, child," she said. "Did you overexert yourself?"

"Yes, I guess I did," Tristaria replied. "Was I asleep for very long?"

"No, not very long at all. The day is not yet through."

"And the prince? How is he feeling?"

"He is feeling wonderful, thanks to you. But I thought it was best for him to stay in bed for the rest of today."

"That's a good idea."

"Now, do you feel like eating? My husband and I will be having dinner shortly, and we would be delighted if you could join us, even if it's only for a little while."

"It would be an honour," Tristaria said.

Esilias looked extremely pleased. "Excellent!"

"But before dinner, there's something I really need to do."

"And what is that?"

Tristaria glanced down at her soiled and sweat-stained tunic. "I really need to take a bath."

"Of course!" the queen said. "I'll have a bath readied for you immediately. And a change of clothes as well."

"Thank you, your highness," Tristaria said.

# TRISTARIA

*Later* that evening, when Tristaria emerged from the bath room, she felt like a completely different person. Not only was she looking very clean and fresh, she was also wearing a beautiful, pale blue sheath dress, with an open back and a long slit. Queen Esilias had given her this dress to wear whilst the keep's servants gave her filthy clothes a good wash. She had not been given any footwear, but this did not bother her. It was quite common to go about in bare feet when indoors in these parts, and she was quite used to this custom.

A servant girl, who was patiently waiting outside the bath room, took Tristaria down a long hallway, to where a large set of double doors were.

"This is the dining hall," the girl explained to Tristaria. "Please go in."

As the girl headed back up the hallway, Tristaria placed her hand on one of the door handles. but before she turned it, she had a self-conscious glance down at herself. She had never worn such luxurious clothing before, so she felt a little awkward in it. But of course there was nothing she could do to change this, so she did her best to put that feeling aside and then opened the door.

As Tristaria had anticipated, the dining hall was quite impressive, befitting that of a royal abode. Along three of its four walls were several murals depicting great battles, as well as a number of statues of legendary heroes. On its fourth wall, the one that faced the entry, there were three large windows, which most certainly provided a great deal of light to the room during the day. But now, with the sun quickly setting, these windows merely provided a dim backdrop and the main light in the room came from a number of wall-mounted oil lamps.

In the centre of the hall there was, of course, a dining table made from stained oak. This table was long enough to comfortably accommodate about two dozen chairs. but only three of them were occupied, all at one end of the table, where a lavish banquet of seafood delicacies had been laid out.

King Galasius was sitting at the head of the table and Queen Esilias was next to him, sitting with her back to the windows, so that they were both more or less facing Tristaria. Only the third person, a youth with dark wavy hair, who was sitting opposite the queen, was not facing her. At first Tristaria thought this person was either a relative or a guest of the king. but the rather old-looking attire he was wearing, plus the fact that he was hanging his head quite low, suggested otherwise.

The queen was the first one to speak. "Please, take a seat, Tristaria," she said.

Before Tristaria could make any sort of response, the sullen youth suddenly straightened, as if he had been struck by lightning. Then he whirled about to look over his shoulder straight at her, his large, grey eyes wide open. Tristaria recognized him immediately.

"Palan!" she cried out, before she could think better of it.

"Trista!" Palantaros cried back, as he vigourously sprang to his feet, knocking over his chair in the process. Then he rushed to Tristaria, nearly knocking her over too, as he embraced her enthusiastically.

"Palan!" Tristaria repeated breathlessly, as Palantaros squeezed her tight.

"I can't believe it's really you!" Palantaros said, but his words were almost indiscernible; he had quite literally buried his face into Tristaria's shoulder.

"Palan, calm down!" Tristaria said. Although Palantaros seemed to have momentarily forgotten where they were, she had most definitely not. She was all too aware that the eyes of the king and queen were on them, and her cheeks reddened. Tristaria tried pushing Palantaros away, gently at first, but when this did not work, she resorted to using force. He eventually released her from his arms.

"What are you doing here?" Palantaros asked her.

"I was going to ask you the same thing," Tristaria responded. "But I think—"

Galasius suddenly cleared his throat loudly, and both Tristaria and Palantaros turned towards him. There was an obvious look of displeasure in his face.

"Please, both of you, take a seat," Esilias said. "We have an important announcement to make."

Palantaros went back to the chair he had upended and righted it, then he offered it to Tristaria.

"Thank you, Palan," Tristaria said and she sat down. Palantaros took the seat next to her.

"Now that the two of you are here," the king rumbled, "I can officially proclaim that I have decided to pardon Palantaros for his crime of burning down my prized orchard."

"Oh, thank you, King Galasius," Tristaria said joyfully. After seeing Palantaros in front of her, she had suspected that the king had forgiven him, so she was not at all surprised by this news.

Palantaros, on the other hand, was once again left wide-eyed in amazement. "What?" was all he could say.

"However, there is a condition," Galasius added, his voice gaining a slightly stern edge. "He is hereby forbidden from ever performing magic tricks in Taraminas again."

Tristaria softly patted Palantaros' hand, which sat on his lap and smiled at him, but he did not move. He was still in shock. Worried that the king might be offended by his lack of response, Tristaria decided to speak on his behalf. "I'm sure Palantaros will abide by that condition."

King Galasius seemed satisfied by Tristaria's words and he turned his attention to the food on the table. Queen Esilias then gestured for Tristaria and Palantaros to do the same, so Tristaria picked up the ceramic plate in front of her. It was the same plate which Palantaros had been sitting in front of when she had arrived at the dining hall, and it was completely clean. Palantaros had evidently been too nervous to even touch the food, let alone try some. Tristaria, though, was quite hungry and she did not hesitate in choosing various morsels of food and placing them on her plate. As she did this, she glanced at Palantaros. He was still looking stunned, but he soon followed her lead and also started choosing things to eat.

# TRISTARIA

*A*fter everyone but Palantaros had eaten their fill, Tristaria asked King Galasius about the murals in the dining hall. Most were of battles fought many years earlier, before Galasius had been born, but there was one that he had been involved in, as a young man, serving under his father. That mural depicted the battle of Agoris, a small port on the northern coast. Back then, several coastal towns of the northern continent were vassals of Lianthia, so when an enemy came down from the far north and threatened them, a united Lianthian army went to their aid. This grand army, of which the soldiers of Taraminas were a part of, landed in Port Agoris, and defeated an army of northerners that tried to intercept it, in what was a decisive victory. But alas, this would be their one and only success. Reinforcements came from the north and drove the Lianthians all the way to the westernmost city on the northern coast. It was there that the Lianthian soldiers and their vassals made their final stand.

"Kaldirion." The name escaped unintentionally from Tristaria's lips.

"Kaldirion," the king repeated. "That's right. It was a massacre. Many good men perished. My elder brother was one of them."

"I'm sorry to hear that," Tristaria said.

The king took a long draught of wine from his goblet and shrugged. "That was all a long time ago," he said, but his voice was quiet and distant.

At this point the queen tried to introduce a new topic. "Tristaria, why don't you tell us a bit about yourself," she suggested.

Tristaria scrunched up her nose. "My life isn't very long and definitely not as interesting as your husband's," Tristaria replied.

"I'd still like to hear about it, if you don't mind."

"Well..."

"You are from the north, are you not?"

"No, actually."

"Oh?"

"I was born in Balanston."

"Balanston? The empty plain on the Rumolin Peninsula?"

"Well, yes, only it wasn't an empty plain at the time. It was a camp."

The king nodded. "A refugee camp, for those who had fled the war in the north after Kaldirion."

"Yes, my father was killed in Kaldirion," Tristaria said, her face suddenly grave.

"And your mother?" the queen asked. "She fled to Balanston alone?"

"She fled with my elder sister."

"And where are they now?"

"They... They both died. My mother when she gave birth to me, my sister when a plague struck the camp. I got sick too, but I managed to recover."

"I'm so sorry, child," Esilias said, her face full of sorrow. "I didn't mean to..."

"That's all right. As your husband said, that was all a long time ago." Tristaria suddenly felt terribly sad, but she fought hard to keep a calm exterior.

"So how was it that you came to be admitted to the Temple of Altaris?" Galasius enquired.

"The camp in Balanston was being run by the Priestesses of Altaris. They treated me very kindly and I decided that one day, I would help other people as they had helped me."

"That is very admirable."

"But that's only part of the story," Palantaros said, speaking for the first time since they had eaten. "Tristaria was also an apprentice to Aldoranis."

Both the king and queen raised their eyebrows. "Is that so?" Galasius said.

Tristaria nodded. "Yes, but only for a short time."

"Well, that certainly explains your incredible skill at magic!" Esilias remarked.

"I still have a lot to learn," Tristaria said. Considering it was Palantaros' careless use of magic that had led to the situation she now found herself in, she thought it best to avoid the subject.

"I was an apprentice to Aldoranis too," Palantaros ventured.

Tristaria involuntarily clenched her teeth, but luckily King Galasius was receptive to Palantaros' words, possibly because of the wine that he had been drinking copiously.

"Tell us how that came to be, young man," the king said.

Palantaros then launched into his tale. Like Tristaria, Palantaros had been an orphan from a young age and had grown up on the streets of the city of Koromil, in the far south of Lianthia. He survived solely by doing odd jobs here and there, for scraps of food.

One fateful day, however, he was waylaid by a group of older boys, who robbed him of a hard-won piece of bread. As the boys ran off, an angry Palantaros picked up a clump of dirt and threw it in their direction. The dirt did not come anywhere near any of the boys, but it did manage to dislodge the tall hat of an elderly man who was coming the other way. That elderly man was none other than Aldoranis.

At first, Aldoranis was furious with Palantaros, but after Palantaros apologized and offered to clean the elderly man's hat, his mood softened. Aldoranis offered Palantaros a job as a servant, which Palantaros gladly accepted, but before very long Aldoranis realized Palantaros had great magical potential and so made him an apprentice.

When Palantaros had finished speaking, Tristaria gave him a quick smile. She now realized he had told this particular tale, which never failed to amuse her, in an effort to cheer her up. And he had certainly succeeded in doing that. The king and queen also seemed to have enjoyed his story immensely.

After a moment of silence, Esilias glanced over her shoulder at the sky outside, which was now dark and dotted with bright stars. "It's gotten quite late, hasn't it?" she remarked.

Tristaria nodded. "Yes, it has. Would it be possible for you to arrange somewhere for us to stay tonight, your highness?"

"Why, you can use the upstairs room you were in earlier. And I'll tell my servants to prepare a room for Palantaros as well."

"Oh, I didn't mean here, your highness. A pair of rooms at an inn will be more than enough."

"Nonsense! I insist you stay here tonight. We are still very much indebted to you for what you did for Losurion today, Tristaria."

# TRISTARIA

*T*he room where Tristaria had spent the afternoon was mostly unchanged, but the bed had been remade and a nightdress had been placed on it. And since the window had been shuttered, a lit candle had been put on the small table beside the bed.

Tristaria picked up the nightdress, which was just as luxurious as the dress she was wearing, and examined it carefully for a few moments, but she had no intention of going to bed just yet. That was because she desperately wanted to talk to Palantaros in private, and she was just waiting for the servant boy who had accompanied Palantaros and herself to the guest rooms to return downstairs.

When Tristaria thought enough time had passed, she blew out the candle and went to the door of her room, which she opened ever so slightly. In the darkened hallway on the other side, there was not a soul in sight.

Tristaria scurried across the corridor and quietly knocked three times on the door of the room Palantaros was in. There were a number of doors in the hallway, but she had earlier taken note of the room that the boy had ushered Palantaros into.

"Who's there?" she heard Palantaros ask.

"Who do you think?" Tristaria answered, in a very loud whisper. "It's me, Trista!"

Loud footsteps hurriedly approaching the door could be heard, before it swung open to reveal the beaming face of Palantaros. He was still dressed as well, but he had removed his sandals.

"Trista!" he cried happily. "I was hoping we'd—"

Tristaria frowned at Palantaros and put a finger to her lips. "Not now, let me in first," Tristaria told him quietly.

"Oh, right," Palantaros said, and he stood aside so that Tristaria could enter, then he shut the door.

Palantaros' room was identical to the one Tristaria was using. It had a feather bed, with a nightgown on it that Palantaros had yet to unfold, and a small table, with a candle set atop it. The candle was still lit, but Tristaria put it out immediately, and the room darkened considerably.

"Why do we need to be so secretive?" Palantaros asked.

"I'm a temple novice now, Palan," Tristaria explained. "It will make me look frivolous if I'm spending time in a boy's room." As she spoke, Tristaria went over to a window and tugged open its shutters. This let the light from the half moon outside to come streaming into the room and onto her upper body, making her exposed skin appear almost radiant.

"That's better," Tristaria said. "Well, Palan, what was it that you were trying to tell me just now?"

"I was just going to say that I had been hoping that we'd get a chance to talk tonight."

"I wanted to talk to you too. That's why I came."

Tristaria remained by the window, so that she could gaze out at the night sky. Meanwhile, Palantaros sat on the floor nearby, with his legs crossed.

"It seems like forever since the last time we were together, doesn't it?" Palantaros said.

"Yes," Tristaria agreed. "You've changed a lot."

Palantaros looked pleased. "So you noticed I'm taller?"

Tristaria grinned cheekily. "Is that what happened? I thought you'd just gotten thinner."

Tristaria and Palantaros then both burst out laughing, but they suddenly stopped when they remembered that they were supposed to be keeping quiet.

After there was no obvious sign that they had attracted any attention, Palantaros spoke again. "You look different too, Trista."

"Well, I guess I'm a bit taller too,"

"And a lot prettier."

Tristaria gave an embarrassed chuckle. "I thought the only one who had drunk wine was the king," she said, trying to brush off the compliment with a joke.

"I'm serious! You look... You look like a princess!"

"It must be because of the dress. Even a log would look like a princess in it."

"No, it's nothing to do with the dress. You'd look just as pretty without it."

Tristaria knew Palantaros was not trying to say anything lascivious, but the words made her blush anyway.

"Oh," Palantaros said, when he realized he had made a poor choice of words. "I didn't mean, you know, that I wanted you to take—"

"I know," Tristaria responded quickly, in an effort to put Palantaros at ease.

Palantaros then tried to change the subject. "How... How have you been?" he asked.

"I've been good."

"So you're still at the Temple of Altaris?"

Tristaria nodded. "I graduate next winter."

"That's great!"

"That is, of course, if I don't get kicked out for leaving the temple without permission."

Palantaros looked aghast. "When did you do that?"

"Two nights ago, not long after Eramaklis told me you were in danger of getting a public beating, of course!"

"Oh, right... So Eramaklis did find you. I was worried he might not. Where is he now?"

"On his way back here, I guess, from Port Kerastes."

"He went to get Miralena too? That's strange. We agreed he'd only go to her if you weren't able to help me."

"Well..." Tristaria said, feeling a slight pang of guilt. "The truth is, Palan, I told Eramaklis that I couldn't come to Taraminas. I only changed my mind after he left for Kerastes. I'm sorry."

Palantaros gave her a big smile. "What are you apologizing for? If you hadn't changed your mind, I'd still be in that tiny dank cell on the outskirts of town. But to be honest, I'm amazed at how easily you were able to convince King Galasius to release me. You must have used some powerful magic!"

"You're right, I did use some powerful magic," Tristaria said. "But probably not the kind you're thinking of."

"What did you do?"

"I'll tell you all the details, but before I do, I want to hear how you got into this mess in the first place. I think that's fair, don't you?"

"Yes, that's fair," Palantaros said. "But it's a pretty long story."

"I don't mind hearing it, if you don't mind telling it."

"Very well, here goes."

# TRISTARIA

*W*hen Aldoranis passed away, which was less than half a year after Tristaria had become a novice at the Temple of Altaris, Palantaros faced an uncertain future. Unlike Tristaria, he had been unable to find a way to continue his magical studies. Therefore, he took Eramaklis' advice and returned to the land of his birth in the south, in order to look for opportunities there, and Eramaklis went with him.

Palantaros spent several months wandering about aimlessly in the south, before joining a travelling circus as an assistant to an elderly magician. For a while, he was glad he had found something to do, but as time went on, he became bored with the repetitive nature of his job. On top of that, the magician never let him take centre stage, despite promises to the contrary. He contemplated quitting the circus several times, but Eramaklis told him that he should only do so if he knew what he was going to do afterwards.

Then, just last spring, Palantaros was approached by a kindly old woman, who said she was in the process of setting up an even bigger circus somewhere on the other side of the Dalgos River. The old woman, who had seen Palantaros on stage a number of times and had been impressed with his magic, offered him a job as one of her circus' stars.

Needless to say, Palantaros was incredibly excited by the idea of becoming a star, but when he talked to Eramaklis about the old woman's offer, Eramaklis was skeptical. Palantaros, however, was determined to join the old woman's circus and so one night he packed up his belongings and without telling anybody, not even Eramaklis, he left the circus to set out eastwards with the old woman. But on the first night they camped out, the old woman vanished, taking Palantaros' magical staff with her. He had been duped.

For the rest of spring and most of summer, Palantaros searched the lands east of the Dalgos for the old woman's circus, but it did not exist and he never saw the old woman again.

Tristaria, who had been listening wordlessly to Palantaros' story all this time, could not stop herself from interrupting at this point. "You mean you no longer have your staff?" she asked, in disbelief.

Palantaros nodded sheepishly.

There was nothing more shameful for a magic-user than to lose their magic staff. Not only did it make them look foolish and irresponsible, it also had more serious implications, especially for an apprentice.

To use magic, a magic-user did not actually need a staff at all. Aldoranis, for example, was famous for never using one. However, a staff did provide two major benefits. Firstly, it allowed a magic user to build-up and store their magic, as Tristaria had done earlier that day, and secondly it helped to focus the magic. Unfocused magic was much weaker and much harder to control. But Palantaros obviously knew all of this, so Tristaria decided not to reprimand him, and instead let him continue with his story.

As summer drew to a close, Palantaros came to the conclusion that he was never going to find his staff without help. But since he was too ashamed to return to Eramaklis or the circus, the only person he felt he could turn to for help, or at the very least some advice, was Tristaria.

And so Palantaros set out on the long journey north to the Kien Archipelago. However, the money he had was not sufficient for him to travel all the way to the Temple of Altaris, and he was eventually forced to work as a street performer, performing flashy magic tricks in front of crowds. This was without a doubt a risky thing for Palantaros to do, but he had no major difficulties. Until he got to Taraminas, that is. There he decided to perform in the main square, but unfortunately it had been a windy day and his magical fireball drifted over the wall of the king's keep. Worried that it would hit the keep itself, he was forced to detonate it low on its trajectory, completely unaware there were trees just behind the wall at that particular spot.

# OF PALANTAROS

Palantaros had been in prison for nearly four days when Eramaklis finally caught up with him, having followed his trail all the way up the Dalgos River. Eramaklis offered to talk to King Galasius himself, but with only a few days left before his punishment was due to be meted out, Palantaros thought it would be better to try and get help from Tristaria, or if that failed, from Miralena, who Eramaklis said was in Port Kerastes.

Tristaria sighed. "You've had a lot of bad luck recently, haven't you, Palan?"

"Yeah…"

"I had a bit of bad luck, too."

"Really?"

"Yes, last night in fact," Tristaria said, then she began to relate her journey to Palantaros. She did not have quite the same talent Palantaros did for telling stories, so she didn't go into too much detail as she recounted all the main events of her journey, but she did include the part where she was robbed.

Palantaros was indignant. "That cretin!" he growled. "We ought to find him and get your money back!"

Tristaria shook her head. "I don't have time for that," she said. "I have to get back to Kien Taril as soon as I can. Besides, even if we did find him, chances are he's already spent the money."

"You're probably right," Palantaros conceded.

Tristaria stepped away from the window. "Well, I guess I should get back to my room now," she said.

As Tristaria walked to the door, Palantaros stood up and followed her.

"Are you feeling tired?" Palantaros asked.

"No, not really," Tristaria responded. "But it's gotten quite late and I'm sure tomorrow will be a very busy day."

Tristaria opened the door and, after checking to see that no-one was in the hallway, she looked back at Palantaros. "I'll see you in the morning," she said.

Tristaria was just about to leave, when Palantaros put his hand on her shoulder. "Wait a moment, Trista," he said.

"What is it?"

"I just wanted you to know how grateful I am that you came all the way here to help me. I swear, I'll never forget it."

Tristaria smiled. "It was no more than what you've done for me many times in the past. Goodnight, Palan."

"Goodnight, Trista."

Tristaria then stepped out of the room.

# TRISTARIA

*The* following morning, Tristaria was awoken by a knock on the door, and she immediately thought Palantaros had come to her room. However, it was not him. It was a servant girl, who had brought Tristaria's garments, now immaculately clean and well-dried, to her room. In addition, the girl brought a message from Queen Esilias, who had invited Tristaria and Palantaros to breakfast.

After Tristaria thanked the servant girl for all her trouble, the girl mentioned that she had knocked on Palantaros' door a couple of times, but had received no response. Palantaros had always been a very heavy sleeper, so Tristaria told the servant girl not to worry about him; once she was dressed, she would go and wake him herself.

Although the sun was up, inside the room it was still dim, so Tristaria went to the nearest window and opened its shutters. Bright sunlight, as well as a cool breeze, came racing straight into the room, bringing a smile to her face. She took a moment to gaze upon the town of Taraminas, as its inhabitants slowly began to stir. But before too long, the fresh air made her shiver a little. After all, she was wearing only a thin nightdress!

Tristaria went back to the bed, where she slipped off the nightdress and put on her own garments, including, of course, her hairband and sandals. And since she was certain that she would be leaving the king's keep after breakfast, Tristaria tidied up the bed and placed the clothes she had borrowed on top of it, neatly folded up, even though it was probably not expected of her.

Now that she was wearing her own clothes again, Tristaria noticed how coarse they felt against her skin and it briefly crossed her mind that it would be nice to have a beautiful dress, like the one she had worn to dinner the night before, if only for special occasions. But whilst she was a novice at the Temple of Altaris, there was little chance she would get any dinner invitations, so she quickly dismissed this idea, picked up her staff, and left the room.

Tristaria had to knock several times before Palantaros came to the door and when he finally did appear, he looked a mess. His hair, which had natural curls, seemed to have grown wild overnight and his eyes were less than half-opened. On top of that, his tattered tunic was full of creases; Palantaros had evidently not bothered to put on the nightgown.

"Trista," Palantaros said, yawning. "Did you forget to tell me something?"

"No," Tristaria replied, puzzled by the strange question. Then she realized what was going on. "Palan, it's morning."

Palantaros rubbed his eyes. "Morning? Are you sure?"

"Of course I'm sure! And the queen has invited us to breakfast. You don't want to keep her waiting, do you?"

Tristaria grabbed Palantaros by the hand and tried to pull him out of his room, but he resisted.

"Hang on, let me put my sandals on," Palantaros said. Then he hurried back into his room.

"Do it quick!" Tristaria called out after him. And he was quick. In fact, he was too quick. When he reappeared, he had only managed to put on one sandal and was struggling to put on the other.

Tristaria sighed. "I think you'll be able to walk better with both sandals on properly, Palan."

"You did say to do it quick," Palantaros grumbled quietly, but he knelt down and did as Tristaria had suggested.

"Yes, but that's not the same thing as doing it half way," Tristaria countered, as she studied Palantaros' unruly locks from above. She was unable to resist trying to fix them up a bit with her free hand, but it proved too difficult a task, so she gave up. Meanwhile, Palantaros continued working on his laces.

Tristaria soon became impatient. "Why are you taking so long to tie up one sandal?" she asked.

"I had to undo the knot first," Palantaros explained, as he stood up. "But I'm ready now."

"Then come on!" Tristaria said, and she led Palantaros down the hall, to where the stairs to the lower floor were located.

Without a servant to guide them, Tristaria was a little worried that they would have trouble finding the dining hall on their own, but luckily Queen Esilias was waiting for them outside the dining hall's entrance, with Prince Losurion at her side. The young prince was looking healthy and happy, and quite entirely different from the day before. King Galasius, however, was not present.

"Unfortunately, my husband won't be joining us this morning," Esilias explained. "He has to deal with several pressing matters that he had put aside while Losurion was ill. But I thought I would take this opportunity to introduce you to my dear son properly."

"Greetings, Prince Losurion," Tristaria said brightly, and Palantaros repeated her words.

"Hello," the boy said bashfully.

"I'm glad to see you are back on your feet so quickly," Tristaria remarked. "You must be a very strong boy!"

The young prince smiled at Tristaria, but he quickly averted his gaze away from her to the floor.

Upon seeing this, the queen gave a chuckle. "He's always quiet around people he doesn't know very well," she explained to Tristaria. Then she looked down at her son. "Losurion, this is Tristaria and her friend Palantaros. I'm sure you haven't forgotten Tristaria. She's the wonderful young healer who helped you get better yesterday. Now be a good boy and say thank you to her."

"Thank you, Tistria," Losurion said, in a tiny little voice.

"Think nothing of it," Tristaria responded.

"Now then," Esilias said. "Let's all have something to eat, shall we?"

# TRISTARIA

*The* dining table had been arranged similarly to the way it had been arranged the previous night, only now the bountiful feast consisted of an assortment of wild fruits and bread. Tristaria and Queen Esilias ate in a leisurely fashion, as they discussed various lighthearted topics. Palantaros and Losurion, however, were soon in an unspoken but fierce competition to be the one to eat the most food as possible. In the end, it was Palantaros who lost.

After breakfast was over, the queen leant over towards the young prince and whispered something to him; it was some sort of instruction, but Tristaria was unable to hear what it was. Losurion nodded and darted out of the dining hall.

"He certainly has a lot of energy!" Tristaria noted.

"Yes," the queen agreed. "He will be just like his father."

Esilias then asked Tristaria and Palantaros their plans for the immediate future.

"Well, I have to return to my temple on Kien Taril as soon as I can," Tristaria replied. "I've been away from it for about three days now."

"I'm going to Kien Taril too, with Trista," Palantaros said.

Tristaria looked at Palantaros in surprise. "What do you mean you're coming with me?"

"Well, you snuck out of the temple to help me, so I thought the least I could do was speak to the high priestess on your behalf. That way you might not get punished."

Tristaria glared at Palantaros. He had inadvertently divulged her secret.

"You left without permission?" Esilias asked.

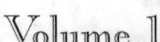

Tristaria lowered her eyes and nodded. She was unsure what the queen would think of such an act. However, Esilias did not seem at all concerned by this revelation. "In that case, I think what Palantaros says is a good idea," she opined.

Tristaria quickly shook her head. "No, there's no need for him to do that," she said. "I can explain things a lot better than he can." Numerous were the times that Palantaros had tried to help her, only to end up making things worse.

"Would you like me to write a letter to your mistress and explain what you did for my son?" the queen inquired. "That may be helpful."

Tristaria waved the suggestion away. "No, no. There isn't any need for that. But thank you for your consideration." It was bad enough that she had snuck out. If the high priestess found out she, a mere novice, had been using powerful healing magic without supervision, she would really be in trouble. She knew of novices who had been expelled for such acts.

Much to Tristaria's relief, the queen did not press the matter. "I understand," she said with a smile. "I'm sure you know what is best for you. So how will you get back to Kien Taril?"

"By boat. The one that leaves this afternoon."

"Don't worry, the docks are only a short walk away from the keep, so you have plenty of time."

"Actually, your highness, the boat to Kien Taril doesn't leave from Taraminas, it departs from the northern docks..."

"The northern docks? Dear me! Then you had better get going!"

Esilias stood up and Tristaria and Palantaros did the same. As the queen started walking to the dining hall's doors, Tristaria went to collect her staff, which she had left standing against the wall nearby. Palantaros, however, followed Esilias.

"Um," Palantaros said, making the queen turn and look at him.

"What's wrong, young man?" Esilias asked.

"When I was imprisoned, I had a small bag with my belongings…"

"Yes, I know. Losurion went to fetch it a moment ago and I think I hear him coming back now."

Sure enough, only a short moment later, the young prince reappeared. He carried a weathered leather bag with him, but Tristaria noticed that he was also carrying a large pouch.

After being prompted to do so by his mother, the young prince handed the bag to Palantaros, who eagerly accepted it. Palantaros then wasted no time in checking his bag's contents.

Tristaria could not stop herself from grimacing and she silently wished that Palantaros had had the sense to wait until they had left the keep to open his bag. Queen Esilias could easily take offence at such an act; it suggested Palantaros did not trust her or her household. Furthermore, Tristaria doubted that there was anything in Palantaros' bag that was worth stealing in the first place.

The queen, however, ignored Palantaros completely. She took the pouch from Losurion, and handed it to Tristaria.

"What is this?" Tristaria asked, even though it was obvious to her now that the pouch contained a large number of coins. And they were probably not copper ones.

"A token of our gratitude," Esilias explained.

Tristaria opened the pouch and sure enough, it was full of gold coins. She bit her lip. She could not recall having held so much money in her hands before, but she knew what the right thing to do was.

"I… I cannot accept this," Tristaria said to the queen. It was at this point that Palantaros, who had quickly forgotten all about his precious belongings, pinched Tristaria's side discreetly. Tristaria shot him a quick glare and said, "A temple healer never accepts payment for their work." Tristaria was addressing Esilias, of course, but her words were also for Palantaros' benefit.

"But surely you spent your own money in travelling here," the queen argued.

"Yes, I did," Tristaria said. And on top of that she had also been robbed, she mused to herself.

After giving it a bit of thought, Tristaria took out a single gold coin from the pouch and showed it to the queen.

"I will accept this, most gratefully, to cover our travelling expenses," Tristaria said and then she handed the pouch back to Esilias, who could not hide her surprise. "Please give the remainder to your town's temple," Tristaria instructed. "I'm sure they will know how to make good use of this money."

The queen nodded. "Very well, Tristaria."

# TRISTARIA

*B*y the time Tristaria and Palantaros left the king's keep, via the front gates, Taraminas was already full of people and activity, much as it had been the previous morning. This made it quite a struggle to walk in anything close to a straight line, but Tristaria did her best as she led Palantaros through the noisy multitude of people thronging in the main square.

"Unbelievable..." Tristaria heard Palantaros mutter.

"There'll be a lot less people once we get out of this square," Tristaria responded.

"I wasn't talking about the crowd, I was talking about the money! It's unbelievable you didn't accept the queen's reward."

"I told you, Palan. A temple healer never accepts payment for their work, Besides, the important thing is that you got released, isn't it?"

Palantaros let out a long sigh. "I suppose you're right. But you could've at least taken two coins, one for you and one for me. I'm really short of money at the moment."

"Don't worry, Palan. I'll split the coin I've got with you."

"But how? With an axe?"

"Of course not. There's a much easier way. We'll buy something."

"Such as...?"

Tristaria stopped suddenly in front of a fish stall. Palantaros was baffled. "A fish? You're going to buy a fish? But we just ate!"

Tristaria ignored Palantaros and turned her attention to the fish on the table in front of her. Most of the stall's stock had already been sold, so she simply looked for the largest fish that was left and pointed to it. "That one, please," she said to the fishmonger, who was a tall and burly middle-aged man.

"Right-o," the fishmonger responded. "That'll be four copper pieces."

Tristaria handed over her shiny gold coin and the fishmonger gave her a pile of copper and silver pieces in return, which she could barely hold in her free hand.

"Here, put these into your bag," Tristaria said to Palantaros and passed the coins to him. Then she picked up her fish by the tail and left the stall.

Palantaros, who was still very perplexed, scampered after her. "You're not going to eat that fish just like that, are you?" he asked.

"Some people do But I'm not going to eat it. I'm going to give it to a friend."

"A friend? A friend other than me?"

Tristaria did not answer this question. She simply smiled coyly, and continued walking across the square, in the general direction of The King's Pride. But of course her true destination was not the inn itself; it was the bush in the narrow alley beside it.

Using her staff for support, Tristaria squatted down right near the bush and lay the fish on the ground in front of her.

"What is this all about?" Palantaros asked.

"Just watch and you'll find out," Tristaria replied.

A few moments later, the cat Tristaria had met two days earlier emerged from the shadows of the alleyway. It cautiously approached the fish and, after taking a few cautious sniffs at it, started eating it ravenously. Tristaria smiled.

"How did that cat become your friend?" Palantaros asked.

Tristaria stood up. "She kindly shared her home with me the other night," she explained.

Palantaros was stunned. "You spent a night in this alley?"

"I had no choice. I got robbed, remember?"

"Gee, and there I was grumbling about the conditions in my prison cell. But at least that had a bunk."

Tristaria and Palantaros then crossed the square again, this time in the direction of the town gates. However, they had not travelled very far when Palantaros abruptly stopped.

"What's wrong, Palan?" Tristaria asked, as she also came to a halt.

"Look over there," Palantaros said, pointing roughly towards the morning sun, which had already risen above even the tallest buildings of Taraminas. "Is that who I think it is?"

Tristaria looked carefully, but there were so many people about that she could not tell who he was referring to. "I... I can't see anybody I recognize," she said after a moment.

"Not on the ground," Palantaros told her. "In the air!"

Tristaria looked again and this time, she spotted a dark, bird-like shape that was flying low, just over the heads of the crowd. But it was not a bird: it was a very familiar faerie-gryphon.

"Eramaklis!" Tristaria cried out. "He must have just arrived from Port Kerastes."

"And it looks like he's headed towards the town's prison," Palantaros noted.

"He's never going to see us in this crowd."

"He will if we catch his attention with some magic!"

Palantaros raised his arm and opened his mouth to recite an incantation, but before he could utter a single word, Tristaria pulled his arm back down. "No, Palan! Have you forgotten what King Galasius said yesterday already? You're forbidden to use magic in Taraminas!"

"Oh, yeah," Palantaros said, and the smirk on his face told Tristaria that he had indeed forgotten.

"Let me do it," Tristaria said.

Tristaria raised her staff and whispered a short incantation. Her staff's power crystal lit up, and a small, luminous orb flew up into the air, where it burst, like a soap bubble, in a bright flash of light. However, since it was daytime, nobody seemed to notice it. Except for Eramaklis, that is. The faerie-gryphon suddenly climbed high into the air to slow himself down, then he turned back towards the origin of the light. His keen eyes spotted Tristaria and Palantaros instantly.

"Well, what an unexpected but delightful surprise it is to see you both!" Eramaklis exclaimed, as he gracefully alighted onto Palantaros' outstretched forearm. "How did you manage to get out of prison, Palantaros?"

"It was all thanks to Trista. She was the one who freed me."

"Is that so?"

"Yes, and it's a great story. Go on, Trista, tell Eramaklis about your adventure."

Tristaria balked at Palantaros' suggestion. "It wasn't really an adventure, it was..." she began to say, before trailing off.

"Even so, I'd certainly like to know what transpired after our last meeting," Eramaklis said, encouragingly.

"And don't you think it'd be a nice way to pass the time while we walk to the docks?" Palantaros coaxed.

Tristaria sighed. "All right, you two win."

"Great!" Palantaros said. "But this time don't leave out the part about the cat."

# TRISTARIA

*By* the time Tristaria had finished recounting her adventure in its entirety, including the part about the cat, she and her companions had left Taraminas and were well on the way to the northern docks.

"So now I have to hurry back to the temple, and hope that I don't get into too much trouble," Tristaria said to Eramaklis, as a way of wrapping up her tale.

"I'm sure your mistress will be understanding," Eramaklis said. "Acts of kindness should not be punished."

"And what about you, Eramaklis?" Tristaria asked. "How was your journey?"

"The journey went well. But unfortunately other things did not."

"What do you mean?"

Eramaklis then went into great detail about his trip to Port Kerastes, starting from when he had parted company with Tristaria. The weather was favourable, so he made good time, and after flying all night, he arrived in Kerastes not long after sunrise. He immediately began to look for the apothecary where Miralena worked, but since he did not know what it was called, he was forced to visit every potion shop he came across. When that proved fruitless, he began asking the locals for any out of the way shops that he might have missed, and he visited those too.

By noon of the following day, Eramaklis had visited dozens of shops, but he had yet to find even a single trace of Miralena. He was just beginning to wonder if she had ever even come to Port Kerastes in the first place, when, upon leaving one shop, he overheard a conversation between two very old men. One of the men was telling the other that he had had to walk for five blocks to buy medicine from this shop, because the apothecary he had relied on for most of his life had burnt down three days earlier. Eramaklis thought it would be a very unlikely coincidence that the shop that the man was talking about was the very one he was looking for, but he asked the man about it anyway.

The old man was quite friendly and quite helpful. He had been a longtime customer of the apothecary that had burnt down and therefore he knew quite a lot about it. Eramaklis asked him if he had ever met someone named Miralena there, and he said he had. According to the man, Miralena had been a very cheerful and helpful young woman and he was sorry that he would no longer be able to chat with her. However, he could not say what had become of her or any of the other shop's staff. He only knew that, thankfully, no-one had perished in the fire.

After asking the old man for directions to the spot where Miralena's apothecary had stood, Eramaklis headed there immediately. As the old man had described, the shop had indeed burnt down, and very little of it was left standing. The building on the apothecary's right, a bookstore, had also been extensively damaged, but the one on its left, a grocery store, was largely unscathed, perhaps by virtue of it being located upwind of the fire.

The grocery store was open, so Eramaklis went there to make some enquiries. From the store owner he learned that the potion shop had had a dormitory on its second floor, where workers who came from other towns could stay. After the fire, most of these workers had moved to a nearby inn, where they intended to work out what they would do next, now that they had lost their jobs.

At the inn, Eramaklis found two workers still there. Unfortunately, Miralena was not one of them, and the only thing the workers were able to tell him was that they had seen Miralena just after the fire had been put out, but they had not seen her since.

Eramaklis was obviously worried for Miralena, but by this time, it was late on the second day after he had spoken to Tristaria, and he decided he needed to head back to Taraminas, so he could offer whatever aid he could to Palantaros.

"I do hope Miralena is all right," Tristaria said, once Eramaklis had finished speaking.

"Did you find out what caused the fire?" Palantaros asked Eramaklis.

"A disgruntled customer," Eramaklis replied. "Or at least, that was what the people at the grocery store assumed, But I'm not so sure. I fear the real reason is something more sinister."

"Such as what?" Tristaria asked, feeling sightly uneasy.

"It's just a suspicion I have, nothing more," Eramaklis admitted. But Tristaria knew that the faerie-gryphon's instincts were rarely wrong.

After Eramaklis' sombre story, the trio spent the remainder of the journey to the docks talking about the past and the happy times they had spent together whilst living in Aldoranis' tower. This certainly helped lift their spirits and almost before they knew it, they had arrived at the northern docks, where people were already starting to board the boats out of Kien Sifel.

"We just made it," Tristaria observed.

"Yes," Eramaklis agreed. "It looks like the boats will be leaving very soon."

Tristaria turned to Palantaros. "Give me some coins, Palan, and I'll go and buy the tokens."

Palantaros pulled a number of coins from his bag and handed them to Tristaria. "Is that enough?" he asked.

Tristaria quickly counted the coins and nodded. "Yes, plenty. Now, what token should I get for you?"

"Kien Taril, of course. So I can go and talk to your mistress."

"Palan, you know there's no need for you to do that. I can handle things by myself just fine. And besides, don't you have more important things to do?"

"Er... Like what?"

"Like going to look for your staff! Or have you given up on that for good?"

"No, but..."

"But what?"

"Well, since I'm here in the Kien Archipelago, couldn't I at least go and see the place where you're studying...?"

Tristaria sighed. With the boats moments away from departure, there was no time for any sort of discussion. "All right, I'll get two tokens for Kien Taril" she said. "But you have to promise me that once you've seen my temple, you'll go back to the mainland and look for your staff."

Palantaros nodded enthusiastically. "I promise."

# TRISTARIA

*It* was evening by the time Tristaria and her two companions silently started up the road towards the village of Velsin, on Kien Taril. The boat trip had been a pleasant and uneventful one, although Palantaros had started to feel a little queasy towards the end. Once they were back on solid ground, however, he soon felt better.

Unlike when she had left Kien Taril, three days earlier, Tristaria saw no point in avoiding Velsin; there was no way her absence had not been detected by now. But as they traversed the main dirt road through the small village, she began to feel unsettled. There were hardly any people about, even though it was still well before nightfall, and there seemed to be an unusually large number of soldiers on patrol, all of them with serious expressions on their faces. The few villagers that were about talked amongst themselves in low, hushed voices.

"Something's not right," Tristaria muttered with a frown.

"I sense it too," Eramaklis agreed.

"Everyone seems scared," Palantaros remarked.

When the trio reached the far side of Velsin, an old man working in his small plot of land called them over.

"You're not headed for the temple, are ya?" the villager enquired.

"Yes, we are," Tristaria replied. "Why?"

"I think you should stay away from there, for at least a day or two," the old man cautioned.

"Has something happened...?" Palantaros asked.

"Yes," the villager replied. "The temple was attacked yesterday, and the culprit hasn't been caught yet."

Tristaria did not need to hear another word. She took off in the direction of the temple, as fast as her legs could carry her, paying no heed to the shouts of the old man and her companions that rang out loudly behind her.

As she raced along the road into the woods, Tristaria prayed and prayed to Lady Altaris that there was some sort of mistake, that there had been no attack, but deep down in her heart she knew that she was praying in vain. Something bad must have happened; there was no other possible reason for the presence of extra soldiers in Velsin.

When Tristaria reached the temple gates, they were only partly open, and there were four soldiers guarding them. One of the soldiers showed Tristaria his palm. "The temple is temporarily closed to visitors," the soldier declared.

"But I'm not a visitor," Tristaria told him. "I'm a novice."

The soldier looked at Tristaria doubtfully, but said nothing.

"If you don't believe me, go and speak to High Priestess Lusianis. Tell her Tristaria wants to return to the temple."

"I can't do that, I'm afraid. The high priestess is not seeing anybody at the moment."

"Well, speak to Senior Priestess Araliana or Senior Priestess Erimaris. They will know who I am."

The soldier pondered Tristaria's words for a long time. "Wait here," he said finally, then he stepped into the temple.

Not long after, Palantaros and Eramaklis joined Tristaria before the gates. One of the three remaining soldiers warned all of them to keep their distance.

"What's going on?" Palantaros asked Tristaria in little more than a whisper.

"They don't want to let me in," Tristaria informed him.

Before they could discuss things any further, the soldier who Tristaria had spoken to reappeared. He was surprised to see Tristaria was no longer alone.

"Who are these two, then?" the soldier asked.

"My friends," Tristaria told him.

"Well, they definitely can't go in. You, however, can. Senior Priestess Araliana is waiting for you inside."

"Thank you," Tristaria responded. Then she turned to Palantaros. "I'll go and find out what's going on."

"We'll wait right here," Palantaros said, and Eramaklis nodded.

Walking quickly past the group of soldiers, Tristaria entered the temple and as she crossed the temple's forecourt, she saw Senior Priestess Araliana, a thin, middle-aged woman with short brown hair, hurrying towards her. Before Tristaria could say anything, however, the senior priestess, was right in front of her.

"My dear child!" Araliana cried, as she gently placed her hand on Tristaria's cheek. "Where have you been?"

"I'm very sorry," was all Tristaria could say, suddenly becoming a bit teary-eyed.

"Thank the Lady you're unhurt," Araliana said, with a clear look of relief on her face. "After the attack, we feared the worst!"

Tristaria swallowed hard. "So it's true? There really was an attack?"

"Yes, last night," Araliana replied.

"Was anybody hurt?"

Araliana paused a moment before answering. "I think I should let the high priestess tell you what happened."

# TRISTARIA

*From* the forecourt, Araliana led Tristaria through the hospice area of the temple, where the sick and injured of Velsin and the neighbouring islands were housed during their treatment. Everything looked perfectly normal here. Priestesses and novices were going about their daily routines without fuss, and although a few girls cast Tristaria a curious glance as she passed by, nobody spoke to her.

In the main courtyard, however, it was a different story. Here, there were clear signs a magical battle had taken place. There were large black holes all over the grass and there were also scorch marks on the walls of several buildings, in particular the Novices' Quarters and the storeroom. But Araliana offered no explanations and simply led Tristaria directly into the Priestesses' Quarters.

Tristaria had fully expected to see the high priestess to be in her study, busy working at her table, just like she had been the last time they had met. But there was no-one in the study and Araliana took Tristaria straight to the rear of the high priestess' room, where the sleeping area was located. The high priestess was there, resting in her bed, with both the right part of her face and her right arm heavily bandaged.

"High priestess!" Tristaria cried out, unable to contain her shock, and tears began running down her cheeks.

Lusianis opened her uncovered eye, and when she saw Tristaria next to her, she smiled. "Tristaria!" she said softly. "Thank goodness you're all right."

Tristaria dropped to her knees and, after putting her staff down, placed both hands onto the bed, so she could lean closer to the old woman's face. By now, she was crying almost uncontrollably. "What...? Who...?"

"Calm yourself, child," the high priestess said. "I may be hurt, but I will recover. So save your tears!"

It took her a little while, but Tristaria managed to bring her emotions under control. Only then did Lusianis respond to her half-formed questions.

"A man came," the high priestess explained.

"What sort of man?"

"A short stocky man, with long dark hair."

"A wizard?"

"Yes, a wizard. A powerful wizard. The other priestesses and I managed to drive him off, but not before he did quite a bit of damage to the temple. A few of us were hurt, but fortunately nobody was killed."

"How did he get in?"

"He had a winged steed. A manticore."

"A manticore..."

In present times, manticores were extremely rare creatures; in fact, Tristaria had never seen one herself. However, she vaguely recalled hearing a story about a manticore a long time ago, when she was still a student of Aldoranis. But it was only a fragment of a memory and nothing very clear.

"The man was after you, Tristaria," Lusianis revealed.

Tristaria was stunned. "Me? How do you know?"

"He was asking for you. He looked for you in the Novices' Quarters and he also searched the storeroom. Anybody who confronted him, he attacked. But he eventually withdrew. He probably realized you weren't here."

"What would a wizard want with me?"

"I do not know. My guess is that you either have some knowledge or an object he needs."

"But I'm just a young girl. I doubt I have any information a wizard would need. And there is absolutely nothing in my possession that is of any value."

"Are you sure about that?"

"Well, yes."

"What about your staff?"

Tristaria glanced down at her staff on the floor. "You think he was after my staff?"

"As I said, I don't know what the wizard wanted with you," Lusianis said. "But it would be foolish to discount any possibilities."

Tristaria frowned, completely lost in thought. As much as the notion frightened her, what Lusianis had said made sense. Her staff had belonged to the very powerful mage Aliania for many years, and as a result, it had been imbued with some of her power. This imbued power was of enormous benefit for a young magic-user, such as herself, provided they were able to tap into it. But for an already-powerful wizard, there would be hardly any benefit, if any benefit at all.

"Where did you run off to, Tristaria?" the high priestess asked, suddenly bringing the young girl out of her ruminations. "You went to Taraminas to help that boy, didn't you?"

Tristaria nodded slowly. "I'm sorry I disobeyed you, mistress."

The old woman chuckled softly. "To be honest, I was furious with you when I was told you'd disappeared. I told myself that when you got back, I would give you a stern talking to. A very stern talking to. But after what happened last night... I'm glad that you weren't here. If you had, you might have been killed. I believe that it was Lady Altaris' will that made you go to Taraminas. She protected you from danger."

"Will... Will I be allowed to resume my studies here?" Tristaria enquired.

"Of course! But not now."

"Why not?"

"My child. That man who came looking for you is still out there. I am almost positive he will come for you again."

Tristaria shuddered. "So what should I do?"

"I do not believe you should seek to confront him. At least, not on your own. He is too powerful for you. Perhaps... Perhaps the best thing to do is for you to go into hiding."

"For how long?"

"I am not sure. But at least a year."

Tristaria felt terribly confused, but she knew she needed to consider this matter very carefully. And she would also need to ask Palantaros and Eramaklis for their advice.

# TRISTARIA

*T*ristaria sat, uncloaked and unshod, atop a grassy knoll in the woods, not much further than a stone's throw away from the eastern wall of the Temple of Altaris. From this vantage point, the vast northern sea was visible. In fact, during the day, it was possible to see the thin line of the northern continent if the weather was clear. But now it was night, and even with the half moon and stars shining brightly in the sky, the black waters of the sea appeared to recede into nothingness.

Palantaros and Eramaklis were both with Tristaria; Palantaros lay on the grass next to her, chewing on a blade of grass, with his hands behind his head, while Eramaklis was sitting close by. Tristaria had already told them what the head priestess had told her and she was now waiting on their responses. Around them, all was tranquil. It was so tranquil, in fact, that it was very easy to forget that just a day earlier the temple had been in utter chaos. Within Tristaria, however, there was nothing but turmoil.

Many moments passed in silence until Tristaria could no longer bear it. "So do you think I should do as the high priestess suggested?" she pressed her friends.

"I think she's right about not confronting the attacker," Palantaros said. "He seems very dangerous. But where could you hide?"

"I don't know. Somewhere far from here, I suppose."

"Such as...?"

"Maybe somewhere in the far north...?"

"That certainly is very far."

Tristaria nodded, but said nothing.

Palantaros looked at Eramaklis. "What do you think?"

"I fear that this problem has no clear solution," Eramaklis replied. "Especially since we know very little about the attacker."

"We do know he rides a manticore," Palantaros ventured.

"Yes, that's right," Tristaria said. "When the head priestess told me about the manticore, I got the funny feeling that I'd heard someone talking about them a long time ago. Someone like Master Aldoranis, perhaps. Do you remember him talking about manticores, Palan?"

Palantaros thought for a while, but in the end he shook his head. "No, sorry."

"Neither do I," Eramaklis said. "However, Master Aldoranis was a great scholar as well as a wizard, so I would not be surprised if he had talked about those creatures in passing at least once."

"Maybe that's what I'm remembering," Tristaria said, disheartened.

Palantaros sat up suddenly. "Hold on a moment!" he cried.

"What?" Tristaria responded, startled.

Palantaros looked at Eramaklis. "The shop that Miralena had been working at burnt down three days ago, right?"

Eramaklis nodded.

"If you ask me, that's a big coincidence."

"Do you think what happened at Miralena's shop might be connected to what happened here?" Tristaria asked.

"It's certainly a possibility worth investigating," Eramaklis opined.

"Oh, but wait," Palantaros said, his excitement suddenly tempered. "Miralena disappeared, didn't she? Who knows where she is now."

"My guess is that she's back home with her mother," Tristaria said. "Her mother was still alive when she was studying with Master Aldoranis."

"And where was her home?" Palantaros enquired. "Do you remember?"

"I'm pretty sure she was from a town in the eastern lands called Falinos, or something like that," Tristaria said.

Eramaklis nodded. "Yes, I know of a place with that name."

Palantaros clapped his hands together loudly. "Well, that's settled! Off we go to Falinos!"

Tristaria gave Palantaros a frown. "We?"

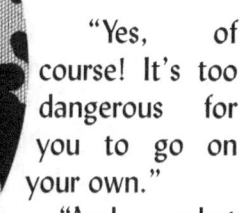

"Yes, of course! It's too dangerous for you to go on your own."

"And what about your staff, Palan? Don't tell me you've already forgotten about it again."

"No, I haven't forgotten about it. But you're more important than any old staff. You're more important than a hundred old staffs!" Palantaros declared.

"I agree with Palantaros," Eramaklis said. "If you decide to look for Miralena, I think we should go with you. But in the end, Tristaria, you need to make the choice that is best for you."

Tristaria raised her gaze to the starlit heavens. "Well, one thing's for sure. I can't stay here. I'd endanger everyone in the temple. And I guess Falinos is just as good as any destination at the moment."

"So it's settled?" Palantaros asked.

Tristaria nodded. "Yes, it's settled. We're off to Falinos."

## Author's Note

Thank you for reading *Tristaria Volume 1: Of Palantaros*. I write this, of course, assuming that you actually have read this book and not simply just opened it here, it's final page.

*Tristaria* is one of my oldest ideas; I do not remember the exact date, but I conceived it in about 1990. Yes, thirty years ago! It was inspired by an illustration that I saw in a gamebook from the *Fighting Fantasy* series of gamebooks (gamebooks were quite popular in the mid to late Eighties). Over time, *Tristaria* has changed a great deal; the plot, the setting and the theme have all changed to some degree. Even the appearance of Tristaria, the titular protagonist, has changed a bit. In fact, quite possibly the only thing that has remained the same over the three decades this book has been in gestation is Tristaria's nature. And I guess that means that this is what's at the very heart of this story.

As stated at the very beginning of this book, *Tristaria Volume 1: Of Palantaros* is the first novella in a trilogy of novellas. The next one will be titled *Tristaria Volume 2: Of Miralena*. However, at the time of writing this, I have no fixed plans to produce this second volume. I will most certainly continue to work on it, because doing creative things is what I live for, but it will not be the only thing I'll work on. Thus it may be quite some time before it sees the light of day. Naturally, this also applies to the third volume. However, this would all most definitely change if Tristaria's story were to receive a lot of interest, as that would inspire me to prioritise finishing volume two (and three, after that). So if you enjoyed this first volume, please let me know! You can contact me via the following email address: contactme@moedimension.com. I also welcome any feeback you may have.

Thank you once again.

*Maruse Rino, December 2020.*

www.ingramcontent.com/pod-product-compliance
Lightning Source LLC
Chambersburg PA
CBHW080942170626
46809CB00009B/3108